Then Cal stood before her. "May I have the honor?"

She stopped clapping. "You?"

He nodded, the dimple creasing his cheek. "Seb and I were declared the co-winners of the wild horse breaking. He's decided to sit this one out with Georgia. What do you say?"

It's not fair, Lord. You know what I have to do. Why do You make it so hard?

"Maggie?" He held out his hand.

A girl could sink deep into those blue eyes and never surface. Her hand went out to his, and she shivered when their fingers touched.

He tugged, and she followed him up onto the platform. Though others moved around them, they were only vague images on the edge of her vision. Cal's face drew her complete attention, and he fitted her into his arms with ease.

His strong hand spread-eagled on her back, guiding her, and her fingers rested lightly on his broad shoulder. He winked at her and tilted his head as if summing her up and liking what he saw.

She couldn't look away. The power he had over her frightened her into stiffening.

"Relax." He leaned in and whispered against her temple, his breath tangling in her hair. "I'm not going to bite you."

You could do far worse than that, Cal McConnell. You could break my heart.

ERICA VETSCH is married to Peter and keeps the company books for the family lumber business. A homeschool mom to Heather and James, Erica loves history, romance, and storytelling. Her ideal vacation is taking her family to out-of-the-way history museums and chatting with curators about local history. She has a bachelor's degree from Calvary Bible College in secondary education: social studies. You can find her on the Web at www.onthewritepath.blogspot.com.

Books by Erica Vetsch

HEARTSONG PRESENTS
HP875—The Bartered Bride
HP887—The Marriage Masquerade
HP900—Clara and the Cowboy
HP907—The Engineered Engagement
HP916—Lily and the Lawman

Maggie and the Maverick

Erica Vetsch

Heartsong Presents

For CJ, who has waited not-so-patiently for Cal's story to be told.

A note from the Author:
I love to hear from my readers! You may correspond with me by writing:

Erica Vetsch
Author Relations
PO Box 721
Uhrichsville, OH 44683

ISBN 978-1-61626-039-2

MAGGIE AND THE MAVERICK

All scripture quotations are taken from the King James Version of the Bible.

All of the characters and events in this book are fictitious. Any resemblance to actual persons, living or dead, or to actual events is purely coincidental.

Our mission is to publish and distribute inspirational products offering exceptional value and biblical encouragement to the masses.

PRINTED IN THE U.S.A.

one

Idaho Territory, June 1884

A handsome man couldn't be trusted, Maggie Davis reminded herself, and a girl would be wise to watch out for the ugly ones, too.

"Last one, Cal." The express office manager pitched her second bag skyward where the driver waited to tie it down atop the coach.

"Good thing. We're almost overloaded." Cal grinned.

Blue eyes, a to-die-for smile, and a dimple. This stage driver was much too handsome to be trusted.

He gave a garbled cry that wrenched Maggie's gaze upward. The contents of her traveling case burst out and cascaded down the side of the stage. Silence fell over the passengers waiting to board, and a pair of lace-edged drawers floated down and draped over the high rear wheel.

Cal grappled with the case. "It just popped open. I'm sure sorry." He grabbed a fistful of corset covers and chemises and stuffed them into the rebellious bag. His attempts served only to loosen the latches on the other compartment of the case.

Petticoats and lacy linen tumbled out and fell onto Maggie's upturned face. She scrabbled and clawed at the flannel and linen, anger surging through her to replace the initial embarrassment.

"Whoa. Look out below." He chuckled. "Looks like you have some faulty buckles here. Let me get those." He lay on his stomach, reached down, and lifted the petticoat from her shoulder.

Maggie snatched it from his hand and found her voice. "Stop trying to help."

Snickers and snorts erupted from the men climbing into the coach.

Cal clambered down with the traitorous luggage banging against the red paint of the coach.

Maggie plucked undergarments from the ground and wadded them together to shield them from prying eyes.

"I'm real sorry, ma'am."

Maggie glanced up and sucked in a sharp breath, caught off guard at his nearness. She stepped back, every muscle tense. "Please unhand my possessions, sir." She grabbed at the clothing in his hand.

They ended in a tug-of-war, a lacy wrapper stretched between them.

He grinned, and his dimple caught her eye. A fine dusting of golden whiskers covered his cheeks and glinted in the sunshine. He stepped closer, the garment going slack between them. "Cal McConnell, ma'am. I do apologize for this little mishap." His husky voice whispered across her skin, making her shiver. "Do you have a name?" He tilted his head to the side and raised his eyebrows. He smelled like soap and starch and the outdoors.

Maggie swallowed. "Davis." She turned away from him, hoping he would get the "keep-your-distance" signal.

"*Miss* Davis?"

She glanced at him and gave a short nod. "That's right."

He blinked, and his dimple disappeared for an instant before he rallied and smiled again. He touched the brim of his hat. "No offense intended, Miss Davis. Do you need help repacking your case?"

"No, thank you."

"Then I'll leave you to it. We'll be pulling out in two shakes." He set her suitcase on the boardwalk and sauntered toward the horses. Maggie stared after him, taking in the way his broad shoulders tapered to his lean waist and how easily his stride ate up the ground.

What's the matter with you? Maggie forced her eyes away from the driver and concentrated on the armful of undergarments she held, stuffing them into the bag every which way. So much for her painstaking packing job of earlier. She'd have to find a set of sadirons when she reached Money Creek.

As she bent to shut the clasps, her necklace slid from her collar and trailed across the battered leather. She straightened and tucked the metal links back out of sight. The necklace reminded her to keep her mind focused on why she was here. She couldn't afford any distractions. Especially not the Cal McConnell kind.

A shout caught her attention. With a clatter of hooves and wheels, a buckboard raced down the street. Several men clung to the seats, and every one held a rifle or shotgun. A cloud of dust swirled around them when they pulled to a stop beside the stagecoach. The men jumped down and formed a circle around the buckboard, facing outward.

Cal rounded the team and approached them from the front. "Bormann, just in time." He let his hands rest on his hips just above his gun belt.

The beefiest of the guards let loose a stream of dark, brown juice. "You know it. Don't get there too early and never get there too late. That's me." He cradled his shotgun across his paunch. "You ready for the transfer?"

Cal flicked a glance toward Maggie. "Soon. Only one more passenger to load." He approached Maggie and held out his hand for her case.

"Who are those men?"

"Nothing for you to concern yourself about. You need to board, miss." He put his hand under her elbow. He opened the coach door and stuck his head inside. "Move over, gentlemen. We have a lady traveling today."

The four men already seated grumbled and shuffled.

Maggie allowed him to assist her. When she settled herself and had rubbed away the tingling spot on her arm where his hand had contacted her, she tilted her head to get a better view out the window.

Two men watched the street while two more lifted a strongbox and walked it toward the stage. They staggered a bit under the weight, and their faces reddened with exertion. Bormann kept his eyes on the box.

Maggie looked to her left in time to see Cal's boots pass the window as he scaled the coach. The stage rocked under his weight. It rocked harder under the weight of the strongbox and Bormann who clambered up past Maggie's window.

One moment they were sitting still, the next the coach lurched and they were on their way. Silver City slid by and disappeared in the distance. Maggie settled into her corner.

Lord, give me strength to do what I need to do, show me what I need to see, and please protect me. I'd sure hate for this job to end like the last one.

≈

Cal leaned forward with the lines threaded through his fingers and spoke to the team. "Get up there."

What was wrong with that girl? Her suitcase coming open was an accident. Surely she could see that. She didn't need to glare at a fellow like he needed a bath. Though the way her little mouth went all prissy was kind of cute, her pulling away from him and looking like she wanted to wipe her hands stung. He shrugged. Why did he care? "Swing along, kids!" He shook up the lines.

The coach went over a rough patch in the road, and Bormann jostled against Cal. "You talk to them horses like they was your children. They're just horses."

Cal climbed the line a little on the near wheeler to cajole him into keeping his mind on his business. "They *are* like children. Every one of them is an individual. Treat them right and they'll run for you until they drop."

"How long you been doing this run?"

"I just started the Silver City to Money Creek run. I was on the Jardin to Money Creek for a while, and I took the Elko run a couple of times, but this is my regular run now. Colonel Bainbridge got me this route so I could be home more often to look out for my sister-in-law when my brother has to be out of town."

Bormann braced his feet and reanchored his hat before spitting off the side of the coach. "And how many times have you been held up?"

The messenger's words chafed like sandpaper. Cal's jaw tightened, and he scanned the scrub along the road. "Three times. Once on every route."

"It's past time we rid the territory of that particular nest of rattlesnakes, isn't it? Seems like nobody's doing anything. The thieves are getting bolder all the time." He gripped the eight-gauge shotgun in his meaty hand. "You're lucky to have lived through three holdups. You heard about what happened to Rivers coming out of Emeraldville? They didn't even bother to tell him to throw down the box. Just shot him right there where he sat. Got away with more than ten thousand dollars in silver and bank notes."

A sigh escaped Cal's lips. "No idea who they are or where they fade away to. None of the money's been recovered."

"I thought maybe once your brother became a U.S. marshal, he might capture these robbers. He did all right catching that kidnapper late last summer."

"The marshals are investigating every lead they can grab hold of—which are pretty few from what I gather. Maxwell has Trace doing mostly prisoner transport these days." He recognized the defensive tone in his voice and tried to pull in his horns a bit.

"I suppose they're all doing the best they can, but no business can stand these losses for long. Not the stage company, and not the mines. That's why I came along this time." Bormann waggled the shotgun. "This here cannon should make any highwayman think twice."

Cal glanced at the box under his feet then at the eight gauge. "You'd better have a pretty good grip on it if you fire from up here. Must kick hard enough to knock you right off the stage."

Bormann nodded before dislodging the wad of tobacco in his jaw and flinging it onto the road. "Who's the pretty bird you helped into the stage? Don't remember seeing her around before."

Pretty bird. That described the woman perfectly. Small and fine-boned, with skin like porcelain. Shiny black hair like a crow's wing, and the brightest blue eyes he'd ever seen. Eyes that had widened in surprise when, like a clumsy oaf, he'd knocked her suitcase wide open right there in the street. The color that had come up into her cheeks reminded him of Rose's after a nap, all pink and warm.

His mouth twisted. Just like a woman to have a whole suitcase of nothing but fripperies and frills. He glanced over his shoulder to the baggage stacked on top of the stage. With the boot full of mail, the top held all the belongings of his five passengers. Miss Davis's two bags sat side by side in the center.

"Said her name was Miss Davis."

"She from around here?" Bormann rubbed his chin then smoothed his hand down his shirt front.

Cal shrugged. "Dunno. She didn't say. I'm not paid to pry into people's business. I'm just paid to get them where they want to go."

Though he tried to sound indifferent, Bormann's questions only heightened the curious thoughts tugging at his mind ever since he first saw Miss Davis in the express office. What was a girl like that doing traveling alone by stage? He'd watch when they got to Money Creek and see if someone met her—family or a fellow or someone. Her touch-me-not expression issued a challenge. Cal loved a challenge.

two

Maggie stepped down onto the main thoroughfare of Money Creek and straightened her cramped muscles. The other passengers retrieved possessions from the driver and drifted away while her own bags remained atop the coach.

"I'll be right with you, Miss Davis." Cal smiled down at her.

Two men with badges emerged from the stage office. The gray eyes and heavy moustache of the taller one caught her attention, as did the easy way he held his rifle. His eyes never stopped moving.

"You're late." He rested his foot on the hub of one of the rear wheels.

Cal rolled his eyes. "Four minutes. There was a little baggage mishap over in Silver City that set me back a bit. Why don't you quit jawing and help me unload? Bormann's getting twitchy." He jerked his thumb to the man who had ridden beside him on the trip. "Don't want that howitzer he's carrying to go off by accident."

Maggie stepped back into the shade of an overhang. Bormann and the marshals escorted the strongbox toward the Money Creek Bank. Plenty of security, but no one on the street seemed to care.

"You want these or not?"

Though the driver now stood beside her, she still had to look up quite a ways to see his eyes. He must be six feet tall. Maybe taller. She never really minded being short herself. In her job, looking frail and unassuming had served her well. "Yes, thank you." She tried to take her bags from him, but he didn't let go. The point of contact between their hands

12

seemed to buzz like tiny bee's wings, and she pulled away.

"Are you being met?" Cal's dimple appeared as the corner of his mouth quirked up. "Or is there somewhere I could carry these for you?"

She shaded her eyes against the late afternoon sun and studied the town. The clock in front of the bank told her she had several hours until her meeting. "Is there someplace I could get supper?"

His grin widened. "There sure is. Why don't you let me treat you? I'd like to make up for dumping your suitcase the way I did." He'd pushed his tan hat back, revealing dark blond hair. The bandana knotted at his throat fluttered. He shifted his weight, put one booted foot on the bench beside her, and propped his forearm on his thigh, casual as a Sunday stroll. An entreating, appealing light sparked in his eye.

How many times had she seen that expression? *"Oh, Maggie, I grovel. Say you forgive me. Let me make it up to you."*

Starch hit her spine. "If you'll please give me my things and point me in the right direction, I won't trouble you any further." She injected her words with as much ice as she could muster.

He smiled as if indulging a petulant child. "Trust me, Miss Davis, it's no trouble at all." He tucked her carpetbag under his arm and took her elbow.

Maggie had no choice but to go along. It was either that or make a scene which would draw far too much attention to herself. Across the street and several doors down, they reached the Rusty Bucket Café. She wrinkled her nose at the eating establishment. The name fit. "Is this the only restaurant in town?"

"You sure do judge the filling by the crust, don't you? Don't let the outside fool you. It may not be fancy, but Georgia serves the best food in the territory." He let go of her elbow and opened the door.

"Mr. McConnell, thank you for carrying my bags, but I can take them from here."

He acted as if she hadn't spoken, holding the door and keeping his jaw tilted at a stubborn angle. With scant grace, she refrained from flouncing on the way past him. His triumphant grin irked her.

Several men sat around one of the tables nursing coffee cups. One raised his cup. "Howdy, Cal."

"Seb, good to see you." Cal set her bags beside the front door.

"Cal, sugar, you've been neglecting me." A large woman wove through the round tables. Maggie could only stare. She'd never seen such a kaleidoscopic conglomerate of colors. Orange curling hair clashed gloriously with a bright green apron spattered with dinner-plate-sized yellow flowers.

Cal didn't seem fazed. "Hey, Georgia. I brought you a new customer. This is Miss Davis. Miss Davis, this is my best girl, Georgia." Cal winked at Georgia. "I'm sorry. She hasn't told me her first name." He quirked his eyebrow at Maggie. "*Yet.*" He turned and hung his hat on the rack just inside the door.

"And she won't if she's as smart as she looks. You're nothing but trouble, Cal McConnell, and well I know it." Georgia grinned and nodded to Maggie. "Pleased to meetcha."

Cal clutched his chest in mock distress. "Georgia, darlin', how can you say that? I thought you loved me." He opened his arms wide in entreaty. His dramatics soured on Maggie.

Georgia's cheeks turned pink, and her eyelashes actually fluttered. To Maggie's amazement, the proprietress patted her aggressive hair and shot a self-conscious glance at the occupied table across the dining room. Georgia elbowed Cal. "Go on with you, you rogue. Miss Davis, I declare, I don't know what this fellow will say next." She bustled toward the kitchen, talking over her shoulder. "I'll bring some fresh coffee."

Cal chuckled and held out a chair for Maggie. She eased onto it and set her handbag on the table.

He circled to his own chair, but instead of sitting on it properly, he turned it so the back touched the table. "Hey, Seb," he addressed the man who had spoken to him when he entered, "how're things at the Double Box?"

"We're rubbing along okay. Place is running over with calves this spring." He dropped some coins on the table and headed toward the door. "Be seeing you, Cal. Georgia, I'll be back for supper before heading to the ranch." His companions rose and left with him.

Cal straddled his chair and turned over the coffee cup on the saucer beside his place setting.

"Have you and Georgia been seeing each other long?" Maggie picked up a menu from the table.

His head came up. "What? Me and Georgia?" He crossed his arms along the back of his chair and glanced over his shoulder to where the last patron was just going out the door.

She shrugged and let her eyes go round and innocent. "You are courting her, aren't you?"

He laughed. "Well, courting might be too strong a word for it. Georgia and I are. . ." He paused, his brows coming together. "We're pals." His smile broadened. "That's it. We're pals."

Maggie tapped her chin with her finger, pursing her lips and studying him. "Pals? Interesting. You should be more careful about the impression you're making on people. If a man called me his best girl and asked if I loved him, I might think he had serious intentions toward me."

His eyes narrowed for a moment then he shrugged. "Georgia understands."

The waitress came back and filled their cups. "You want dinner or just pie?" She thumped the spatterware pot down on a trivet in the center of the table and grabbed the pencil from behind her ear. Digging in her apron pocket, she removed a tablet.

"We'll both have the special and pie." Cal sipped his coffee and stared at Maggie over the rim of his cup.

Maggie lay aside her menu and gritted her teeth. "I will have the special, thank you, but no pie."

Cal set his cup down. "You really should try the pie. My sister-in-law makes them, and you won't find better anywhere. Georgia, bring her a piece of pie."

Her eyes narrowed. For too long she'd allowed a handsome man to push her in directions she didn't want to go. But no more. "I don't want *pie*," she enunciated. "I'm quite capable of ordering my own food, thank you."

He scoffed. "Everybody has pie at the Rusty Bucket."

"I'm not everyone."

Georgia snickered. "No pie for Miss Davis." She scribbled on her pad and bustled toward the kitchen.

"So," Cal broke the awkward silence, "what brings you to Money Creek? Will you be staying, or are you just passing through?"

She crossed her wrists on the edge of the table. "A bit of both, I suppose. Money Creek is on my sales route. I anticipate being a frequent traveler on your stage in the coming weeks." *Or however long it takes to do my job.*

"Sales? You don't look like a peddler. What are you selling?" The corner of his mouth quirked up and that dimple appeared. The way he tilted his head, as if his whole attention hung on her answer, seemed so practiced and smooth she almost rolled her eyes.

"Nothing you'd be interested in."

He leaned forward, and his teeth flashed as he smiled. "We got off to a bad start. I'd like to remedy that. Maybe I could buy something from you, be your first customer as a sort of welcome to Money Creek. What are you selling? Patent medicine? Books? Why don't you try me?"

She shrugged and picked up her cup. "You've already seen most of my inventory."

"I have?"

"Why, yes. I sell ladies' undergarments." Maggie had a hard time not laughing at his bullfrog-that-swallowed-a-pinecone expression.

❧

Just after sunset, Maggie waited in the trees behind the livery stable. A soft breeze chased away the worst of the day's heat and whispered in the leaves of the scraggly tree she leaned against. She had to give Cal his due. The dinner at the Rusty Bucket had been the best she'd had in months—even without the pie.

A twig snapped in the dusk.

"You're losing your touch, Maxwell." She straightened. "I could hear you a block away."

"You need to remember I'm your boss, Maggie, not the other way around." His words held no real reproach. They'd worked together too many times over the past three years to stand on much ceremony. Maxwell jerked his thumb toward his companion a few steps behind, the mustachioed man who'd met the stage. "This is Trace McConnell."

Maggie started. "McConnell?"

Maxwell grinned. "No flies on you. He's Cal McConnell's brother."

"There's a family connection?" Irritation flitted through her chest. "Is that wise?"

"Don't get your dander up. Cal doesn't know about you, though Trace isn't too happy about not telling his brother."

Trace laid his rifle across his shoulders and draped his hands over it, letting them hang from the wrists. "We've been round and round on this one." His voice rumbled in his chest.

"That we have." Maxwell's face grew stern. "For now, we can't trust anyone. Someone is feeding the robbers information. We made a big show today of transporting silver. Bait, and not so much as a nibble." He smacked his fist into his hand. "It's like they know our plans before we do."

Trace's rifle slid off his shoulder. "You can't think Cal is involved in this." Though he didn't raise his voice, the ferocity behind the words sent a shiver down Maggie's spine.

"We have to be thorough with our investigation. Everyone on the Money Creek Stage Line gets the same treatment. Stock wranglers, clerks, drivers. . .everyone. That way when a trial starts, no one can say we played favorites or didn't investigate everyone. I don't want the fact that Cal has a brother in the U.S. marshal's office to compromise the case in any way. We've ruled out most of the employees. They didn't have access to the information, but because the colonel, who owns the line, knows and trusts Cal, he's been privy to more. Cal has stood in for the shipping clerk here in Money Creek upon occasion, and he's been held up on three different runs. No other driver has been robbed that often."

"I'm telling you, you can trust Cal."

Maggie shook her head. "I don't trust anyone. Especially not where money is concerned. At best, money clouds judgment. At worst, it turns law-abiding men into animals."

"Don't take it personally, Trace." Maxwell chuckled. "Sometimes I'm not even sure Maggie trusts me. It's what makes her such a great investigator." He tucked his thumbs into his gun belt. "It's all set for you to stay at Trace's house like we planned. His wife doesn't need to know who you really are either. To her, you're a saleswoman for a clothing company, and nothing more."

Trace scowled. "I don't like lying to my wife."

"Is he always like this?" Maggie blew out a breath and sent a pointed glance at Maxwell. "It does no good for me to maintain a cover if everyone knows who I am." She turned to Trace. "Secrets are only secrets as long as they *stay* secrets. I don't know your wife. I'm sure she's a lovely woman, but my life depends upon the bad guys not knowing who I am. I'd hate to get shot because your wife spilled the beans at her quilting bee."

Trace didn't argue with her, but his glare could start a fire.

She turned back to Maxwell. "What do we know so far?"

"We know the stage line is losing money and the mines are howling for better security. This gang has hit every branch line at one time or another, and every time they've gotten away with the contents of the strongbox. Every time we've laid a trap for them, they seem to get wind of it. Like today. We were pretty overt, but nobody showed even the slightest interest in the stage."

"Who knew the shipment was a fake?"

"That's just it. Not a lot of people were in the know. We kept the circle tight."

"What about the money? Has none of it surfaced?"

"Not any traceable money. We figure they're using the cash for operating money and either stashing the silver or somehow getting it out of the territory."

"How trustworthy is the express messenger—Bormann?"

"Yesterday I would've said he was on the level, but today, I say we follow your instincts and don't trust anyone." Maxwell slipped an envelope out of his vest pocket. "Here's your expense money. Try to go easy on it."

She took the envelope, grateful to get it. The bulk of her last pay packet had gone to paying the final installment on her debt. Debt free, healthy for the first time in months, and on the cusp of a new investigation. She tucked the money into her pocket. "So, while I ride the coach and keep my eyes open, you'll be checking those names?"

"Well, there's a little problem with that." Maxwell grimaced.

"Turns out, both Trace and me have to go to Boise for a trial. We're transporting two prisoners tomorrow morning to be tried for murder up there. We're both testifying, and I'm not sure when we'll be back here. Depends on the docket, I guess."

She let out an irritated sigh. "How are we supposed to conduct an investigation if you're sitting in a courtroom?"

"Aw, Maggie, you know you don't really need me. You've run operations by yourself before."

"Nothing of this magnitude. How much leeway do I have?"

"Anything up to breaking the law. Everything by the book, but get creative if you have to."

"So, the same as usual." She smiled.

"Yep. Be careful using the telegraph. We don't know where the leaks are." He patted her on the shoulder. She tried not to wince at the impact but didn't quite make it. "Oh, sorry, Maggie. I thought that was healed up. Are you sure you're up to this?"

"I'm fine." And she was. Really. The wince was more of a habit these days. She slipped her arms out of her jacket and folded it over her arm. Little of the day's heat had dissipated, even after sundown.

"You're going heeled, right?" Maxwell pointed to her side. "Where's your gun?"

"I can't wear it against the scar. It's still too tender." She pointed to her hem, lifting it to show him the derringer just above her boot top. "I had a special holster made. Don't worry. I never go anywhere without it."

"That peashooter doesn't have much stopping power."

"I doubt I'll be drawn into a shootout on the main street. I can't exactly go toting a shotgun around, and an ankle gun is less likely to be spied, especially if I'm living with Trace's family and traipsing through town selling lace and linen."

After giving her the name of the hotel where they'd be

staying in Boise, Maxwell left them to head back to the jail.

Trace picked up her bags and started for his house. "What'd Maxwell mean about you healing up? What happened to you?" Trace's gray eyes pierced her, evaluating as they walked down a side street.

"I got shot last fall. Actually, it was because of the shooting that your wife ended up going along with you to get her niece back. I was on my way here to join Maxwell for the kidnap mission when the stage I was on got robbed." She touched the spot where the bullet had entered. "It's taken me all this past winter and into the spring to heal up, but I'm better now."

Trace walked along, tall and silent. At last he said, "I'd feel better if it was a man Maxwell was sending in. I don't like the idea of a woman getting shot."

Indignation flared through Maggie. Another male who felt he had to protect her. "Don't worry about me. A man can get shot as easily as a woman, easier sometimes. I'm good at my job. What happened a few months ago was a fluke."

"Some fluke. You get found out, these outlaws won't care if you're a woman. Doesn't that worry you?"

It did, but she'd learned not to let it show. "They should be the ones worried. I can take care of myself." *Just like I always have.*

three

Lily McConnell feathered her fingers through the fluffy, blond hair of the child perched on her slender hip and smiled welcomingly to Maggie. "Pleased to meet you, Miss Davis." She extended her hand.

The picture the woman and child made caused an ache in the region of Maggie's heart. "I really appreciate you renting me a room. I'll try not to get in your way too much."

"Trace tells me you're a saleswoman." Lily handed the tot to her husband.

The little one squealed and reached out to pat his moustache. Trace's eyebrows came down as he slid a look across to Maggie, but he didn't contradict the statement. He buried his nose in the baby's neck and growled, making her giggle and clutch the hair over his ears.

"Yes." Maggie poked her suitcase with her toe. "I'll be traveling a lot between Silver City and Money Creek."

Lily's friendly, open smile made Maggie's conscience twitch. "That's Cal's run. You'll see him often. He's Trace's younger brother, and he's underfoot around here all the time. He loves to visit Rose."

Maggie clamped down her back teeth. Bad enough seeing him on the stage, but to have him hanging around where she boarded? Still, what better way to keep an eye on him and gauge his possible involvement with the robberies? His brother's confidence in Cal's innocence was admirable, but Maggie wasn't going to be fooled into letting her guard down.

Trace pretended to drop Rose, then caught her and returned

her wide grin. "Cal loves your pie, you mean."

Lily laughed and chucked the girl under the chin. Four tiny white teeth showed as she babbled something her parents understood but sounded half-duck, half-chicken to Maggie. The only child of a widowed father, Maggie had never spent much time around babies. She fingered her necklace, allowing the familiar ache to pass, then jerked her attention back to the job at hand.

Boots sounded on the porch steps, and the screen door squeaked. Cal McConnell stepped inside and swept his hat off. He went to toss it onto the rack beside the door but stopped in mid-motion when he caught sight of Maggie. "What are you doing here?" His blue eyes narrowed.

"Calvin McConnell, what's gotten into you?" Lily stepped forward and put her hand on Cal's arm. "Miss Davis is going to be boarding here for the next little while." Her brows came together.

"Sorry." He jerked his chin then looked over Lily's head toward Trace.

Lily raised her eyebrows at him. "I take it you've met Miss Davis?"

"On the stage today."

"Of course you did. How silly of me." She nodded and patted his hand. "As soon as Trace told me he'd found a boarder for us, I knew it was providential. It will be nice to have company. Trace is headed up to Boise in the morning for another trial, and who knows when he'll be back? And since Maggie travels a lot in her work, she can stay here when she's in town and not have to worry about holding a room at the boardinghouse. Everyone wins." Lily dusted her hands as if that settled things once and for all.

Cal hooked his hat on a peg and reached for Rose who leaned out of her father's arms with hands outstretched.

Trace handed over the baby girl and drew Lily toward the

stairs. "I'll take your bags up to your room, Miss Davis."

"Hello there, princess. How's my best girl?" Cal held the baby high.

"Your best girl? I thought Georgia was your best girl."

His blue eyes clouded as if her words puzzled more than hurt him, and he lowered Rose to rest on his forearm. "It's been my experience that people who are suspicious of everybody are usually hiding something. What are you hiding, Miss Davis?"

Maggie crossed her arms and swallowed, unable to hold his stare. He really was a handsome man, even when he frowned at her. His square jaw jutted out, and the baby looked small against his broad chest. The little girl stuck her thumb in her mouth and dropped her head to his shoulder, smiling around her thumb at Maggie.

Get your mind back on the job.

"Do you live here?" Because keeping an eye on him didn't mean she wanted him in the same house.

"No, I have my own place. It's not much, but since I'm only in town half the time, it'll do for now." He headed toward the kitchen. "Lily," he hollered upstairs, "Rose and I are raiding the pie safe."

"Take Miss Davis with you. I'll be down in a minute to get the coffee started." Her voice drifted from the head of the staircase. "Don't give Rose any of that pie. Give her a slice of bread. She's had enough sweets today."

The informality with which they treated each other awoke a longing in Maggie she'd tamped down for too long. A longing for family, to be a part of a group of people who cared about each other, who were easy with each other. She had been alone for too long.

She thrust aside her thoughts. Nothing more fruitless than recalling past regrets.

Cal set Rose in a tall chair in the spacious kitchen and grappled with a tea towel, trying to tie her in. Rose squirmed and slapped her hands on the tabletop, gurgling and jabbering. He finally managed the knot and turned to open the pie safe.

Maggie gasped at the contents. There had to be two dozen pies in there.

Cal turned to look at her over his shoulder. "Any preference?"

"Did she make all these?" Maggie stepped close. Apple, cherry, pecan, peach.

"I told you Lily makes the pies for the Rusty Bucket, and anyone else who cares to order one. She runs a bakery out of her house. Tomorrow Georgia will stop by and pick these up for the café." He lifted out a lattice-topped blueberry pie glistening with sugar crystals. "Ah, my favorite."

Lily entered. "They're all your favorite. If I know you, you stopped at the café for supper and already had a piece of pie tonight."

Cal patted his lean middle and grinned. "I can never get too much of your good pie, Lily, but Miss Davis passed up the chance to have some at supper."

"Not everyone likes pie as much as you do. I won't be offended if she doesn't want a slice." Lily stirred the fire and slid the coffeepot to the front of the enormous black range. "Coffee, Miss Davis?"

"Maggie, please, and yes, I'd love a cup of coffee *and* a slice of pie. It looks delicious." She leveled a stare at Cal. She'd have pie when it suited her.

Trace slipped into the room and slid his hands around his wife's waist from behind. She leaned into him, placing her hands over his, and sighed when his chin came down to rest on top of her head.

Maggie swallowed and pressed her hands together.

Trace squeezed Lily. "Cal, Pa went on another bender last night. He got his hands on a bottle of rye, and when it ran out, he tried to throw it through the mirror behind the bar at the Golden Slipper. He was so far past half-lit, he missed and only managed to break a couple of glasses."

Cal's knuckles whitened around the knife handle. Maggie took the chair beside the baby who banged a spoon. The knife slid through the pie in quick slashes, and Cal served thick, syrupy slices with speed that spoke of practice. "Where is he now?" He set a plate in front of Maggie and didn't meet her eyes. His bored tone pricked her attention. If she hadn't seen his hand tighten on the knife, she wouldn't have thought the news about his father had any effect on him.

"He wouldn't come home with me. Said he was going to his room in the livery. I paid for the damages." Trace let go of his wife and held out a chair for her. "You can look in on him when you go check on your horses."

Cal nodded as if this was a common occurrence. "You should've bunged him into a cell to sleep it off. Did Powers make trouble?"

"Nope. Me and Maxwell have been watching the jail while Powers was over in Jardin. Tomorrow we're headed to Boise. Escorting Blakely and Kruger up there to stand trial." Trace poked his fork into the slice of pie Cal slid across to him. "I'd appreciate it if you'd check in on my girls while I'm gone."

Cal's smile lit the room. He winked at Lily. "She'll have her usual hard time getting rid of me." He straddled a chair and spun his pie plate around to attack the crust first, just as he had at the café.

"Cupboard love." Lily matched his grin. "If I was a terrible cook, I might never see you, you charmer."

❧

Cal escaped the confines of Lily's kitchen, which seemed much too crowded with Maggie Davis sitting there like a statue. What was it about her that got under his skin? And why did she treat him like something she wanted to scrape off her shoe? She would bear watching, especially with her staying in Trace's house and his brother heading out of town. He didn't have any proof Maggie was up to no good, but something about her bothered him.

He strode toward the main street a block to the south, allowing the night breeze to cool his irritation. The tinkling of a piano came from the saloon, and up the way a donkey brayed. Light shone from the Rusty Bucket, open late tonight. Through the window, he saw Georgia bent over a table stacking dishes. No sense heading to his room yet. The noise from the café would keep him awake. Hopefully, by the time he'd finished checking on his team and on his pa, the restaurant would've cleared out.

It was a coin toss on how he would find his parent. He'd either be belligerent and surly or apologetic and weepy. Cal wasn't in the mood for either.

Stable smells wrapped around him when he stepped into the livery, familiar and comforting. He struck a match on a post and lit the lantern hanging from a spike on the wall. Glossy rumps stood in ranks in the stalls. This team of matched bays was Cal's favorite. He made a quick detour into the feed room and grabbed a fistful of carrots.

"Hey there, Doc." He patted a brown haunch and sidled toward the gelding's head. "Did you eat up?" The horse whickered and shifted his weight. A quick check showed the manger half full of hay, the grain box cleaned out, and a fresh bucket of water in the corner. Cal snapped a carrot in half and held it out. Doc whiffed, his breath warm on Cal's palm, and the carrot disappeared.

At each stall it was the same. Eyelids drooped, hind legs tucked under, coats gleamed with brushing. Neat as a pin. Cal made it a practice to check on his horses every night. They worked hard pulling the heavy stage across the hills of southern Idaho Territory. If one of them was ailing, the rest of the team had to work that much harder. The first sign of trouble with a horse usually showed up in the feedbox. A horse that didn't eat was a sick horse.

Up the line Blaze nickered and stamped his foot, impatient for Cal to get there with his treat. Jackie swished her tail, while Rufus snored.

Each horse had its own personality, its own quirks, likes and dislikes, just like people, and Cal found it made for more harmony and an easier trip on himself and the passengers if he knew his team as well as he knew his own family. The other drivers teased Cal about pampering his animals, but Cal had the best route times and the lowest attrition rate on the line.

Satisfied that all was well with the horses, he turned his attention to the harness. It wasn't that he didn't trust the wranglers. He just felt better seeing for himself. He went over every buckle, strap, and rein, looking for cracking or metal that would chafe.

Wrapping up the last line, he admitted to himself he was stalling. God had been working on his heart over the past little while about forgiving his father and showing him the love of Jesus. That sure seemed easy while Cal was sitting in church on Sunday morning, but somehow by Monday, when he had to put some boots on his faith and walk it around town, things got complicated. At those times it was hard to trust God and not let the hurts count for too much.

Angus McConnell slept in the stall at the far end, when he bothered to sleep at all. The livery owner, a drinking crony, gave him a job cleaning stalls whenever Angus was sober enough to hold a pitchfork.

Cal leaned against the partition and rapped his knuckle on the door. "Pa, you in there?"

A rustling sound, followed by a thump. "Go 'way."

Belligerent and surly. *Lord, You're going to have to help me here, because I want to walk away.*

"You all right?"

"Whoz'at?"

"It's Cal. I'm coming in, so don't throw anything at me."

Angus was famous for slinging anything lying around loose at whatever Good Samaritan happened to be trying to help him out. "Leave me alone." The words came out on a long groan.

Cal ignored this and stepped inside. He hung the lantern on the hook beside the door and put his hands on his waist. Stale air and old whiskey mingled with dirty drunk. Sadly, as familiar to Cal as the smells of the stable.

Angus sprawled on a cot, his arm thrown up over his eyes to shield them from the light. A couple of empty bean cans lay on a crate he used for a table, and a burlap sack held his few belongings. Why would a man insist on living in this squalor when he could have a perfectly good home with one of his sons? Familiar frustration clawed up Cal's ribs. "Come on. Let's go."

"I ain't going nowhere."

"I'm not leaving you like this. We'll go back to my place and get you cleaned up and you can spend a night in a decent bed." Cal bent and put his hand under Angus's arm. Anticipating the next move, Cal leaned back to avoid a flailing fist.

"Get your hands off me, you pup."

Cal grabbed Angus's wrist. Gentle suggestions never worked when his pa was hung over. "We're going to my room. You can walk or I can carry you, but you're going either way."

Angus glared with eyes so bloodshot Cal winced. His pupils were enormous, and he couldn't stand on the first attempt. He pressed his palms to his temples and groaned, perched on the side of his canvas cot.

Cal gave him a minute to gather himself then pulled him to his feet.

Angus staggered and swayed, groaning, but he put one foot in front of the other.

Relieved to have him moving in the right direction, Cal reached up for the lantern and clamped his hand on Angus's elbow to steer him out of the barn. Cal only caught a few of the words his pa muttered, but none of them were very nice and a couple would make an outlaw blush. "Knock it off. I know your head hurts, but that's no reason to talk like that."

"Don't tell me what to do."

Everything Cal wanted to say, and would have said just a few months ago, crowded to the tip of his tongue. He locked his jaw to keep from speaking unkind words. "You'll feel better after we get some coffee in you and you get some decent food and some sleep."

They were almost to the Rusty Bucket when Angus made a strangled, gargling sound and leaned over the hitching rail. He heaved, his skinny body wracked with spasms.

"Ah, another charming little McConnell moment, I see." Sheriff Albert Powers stepped out of the saloon and let the swinging doors flop behind him.

Cal pinched the bridge of his nose and squeezed his eyes shut. He forced a bland expression—one he knew irritated Powers—and leaned his hip against the hitching post. "Evening, Sheriff."

Angus heaved again then groaned, cradling his stomach with one hand and swiping the back of his wrist across his slack mouth with the other. He glared at Powers, defiant, but too weak to do anything about it.

"You're making a nuisance of yourself, Angus. Do I need to haul you in for being drunk again?"

Cal helped Angus stand straighter. "No need. I'm taking care of him."

Powers barked out a laugh. "Angus McConnell only comes

one of two ways, drunk or getting over being drunk. Get him off the street." The sheriff threw a scathing sneer at them and pivoted to go back into the saloon.

Angus looked longingly at the Golden Slipper. "I think I'd feel better if I had a beer. You know, sort of the 'hair of the dog that bit me.'"

Gripping his father's elbow more securely, Cal shook his head. "No. No beer." He pulled Angus along toward the café. Though he knew every pore of his father's body cried out for alcohol, Cal wouldn't help him get it.

They entered just as Georgia was pulling the shades and turning down the lamps. Seb Lewis, the last customer of the night, held the door for them. Georgia didn't ask any questions, just took one look at Angus and went to the kitchen to stoke the fire for coffee.

"Make sure the door's locked when you turn in." She patted Cal on the shoulder. If anyone in this town worked harder than Georgia, he didn't know who. She'd be back in less than eight hours to serve breakfast to her customers.

Though Angus drank two cups of Georgia's strong brew, he pushed away offers of food. With a final groan, he laid his head down on the table and fell asleep.

The clock on the kitchen wall chimed eleven when Cal lifted his scarecrow-thin father onto his shoulder and carried him outside and up the back steps to the room he rented from Georgia. Sloping eaves in the attic space meant Cal could only stand upright in the center of the room.

He eased his pa down onto the only chair. With a couple of quick flips, he opened the tarpaulin from his bedroll and spread it over the quilt on the iron bedstead. No chance of getting Angus to bathe tonight, so the canvas would protect the bedding. Cal carried him to the bed and laid him on the mattress. Settling himself onto his bedroll on the wood floor, Cal released a sigh.

A rasping snore came from just over his head when Angus rolled onto his back.

Cal closed his eyes and put an end to a day that had started chewing on him at sunup and hadn't let go.

four

Maggie's travel case thumped against her leg as she walked down Main Street. How she ever let Maxwell talk her into this particular masquerade was a mystery to her. Next time, she'd be a journalist, or a botanist or something. Next time? Perhaps it was time she looked for a new line of work.

The Money Creek Bank, a brick building with a solid, green door and bars on the windows, bespoke money, security, and trust. Maggie entered and hushed busyness surrounded her. Opposite the door stood a long counter with two teller windows, grilled openings in a frosted glass wall that separated the customer from the cash. A wooden half wall with a swinging gate defined the area for customers. Behind the half wall, an impressive desk with neatly squared stacks of paper took up most of the space, and at the back of the bank, a thick metal door stood open. A short man stood on tiptoe to place bundles of money on a high shelf inside the walk-in safe.

Hecker, the bank president. He came out of the vault and closed the door, leaning all his weight into the process. The door made no sound, and after it shut, he spun the lock on the front. He turned and she caught his eye. "Good morning. How may we help you?" His walk had a bounce to it, like a leprechaun or sprite.

She almost laughed as he popped through the gate. Nearly bald, he had several long hairs lying across the top of his head. Maggie smothered a smile. She was at least an inch taller than the banker. At just under five feet tall herself, being taller than a man rarely happened.

He rubbed his small hands together and bounced a little on his toes.

"Mr. Hecker? I'm Maggie Davis. I've recently relocated to Money Creek, and I'd like to open an account."

"Splendid, splendid." He ushered her through the gate and showed her to a seat beside his desk. The contrast between the huge desk and the little man made Maggie smile, but Hecker was all business. He filled out the papers and took her opening deposit.

"Now that I've seen your bank and that vault, I'm comforted to know my money will be in a secure place."

Hecker, unlike some bankers, merely nodded. On more than one occasion while working for Maxwell, Maggie had induced a banker into boasting about his bank and showing her all his security measures. When Maggie revealed who she worked for and how easily the bankers had given up the information to her, those powerful men of business had blushed and stammered like schoolboys. If she could get them to open up like that, what was to stop a bank robber from sending someone in to do the same? But apparently Hecker wasn't cut from the same cloth. Her senses heightened.

He wrote in her savings book in a cramped but legible hand and passed it over to her. "We're always delighted to have new customers. Please, let us know if we can help you in any way."

"Actually, I was wondering if you could recommend a bank in Silver City. You see, I'll be traveling quite often between the two towns, and I don't want to carry much money on the stage. I've heard about the robberies."

Hecker's lids came down a fraction, and he stopped fussing with his vest buttons. "That's probably wise. I can give you the name of a bank manager in Silver City." He took a card from his desk drawer and drew his pen and inkwell toward him.

"When I came into town, there were so many guards when they unloaded the express box. There must've been quite a sum of money in there, enough to tempt many an outlaw, I would think." She leaned a little forward and lifted her brows a bit, inviting him to share what he knew.

He handed her the card with the banker's name on it and picked up a stack of papers, tapping their already square edges. "I have no doubt the law will apprehend the highwaymen soon." His lips pressed together just slightly, and if Maggie hadn't been watching close, she would've missed it.

She exited the bank making mental notes and rehearsing the interview to write down later. These things took time and careful probing. Hecker was a contradiction, always in motion, his demeanor making Maggie think there was a lot going on in that balding dome, and yet, he said very little. Her instincts told her he would bear watching. He was on the short list of people who knew the last silver shipment was a sham, and as a banker, he could move money and hide stolen cash more easily than most.

She made a brief stop at the stage office to purchase a ticket to Silver City for the following day and made the acquaintance of Joe Williams, the lanky ticket agent. "I'm sure we'll be seeing a lot of each other." Maggie slipped the ticket into her bag and pulled the strings tight. "I imagine I'll be in here as often as the express messengers."

Joe smiled and eased the suspender on his right shoulder. "Always happy to meet a regular customer." His Adam's apple lurched like a chicken drinking water. He had a poultry-ish air about him, with his jerky, bobbing motions and bright, small eyes.

"I've heard a lot about the stage robberies lately. Should I be worried? Is the stage line doing anything special in the way of security until these men are caught?"

"Don't you worry. New policy is to have an extra guard

with each shipment. We'll have one on the box with the driver and sometimes even one in the coach itself."

Admirable precautions, but if any outlaw worth his salt was watching, two armed guards on a stage was as good as painting a red X on the express box with a sign saying: Treasure Here. Inclined to think Joe harmless but unwilling to rule anyone out at this early stage, she put him in the maybe column on her mental list.

When she stepped onto the sidewalk, she ran smack into a formidably-faced woman in black bombazine. "You're the garment sales girl?" Her dark eyes took Maggie's measure, and from the way the woman's lips pinched, Maggie assumed she'd come up lacking.

"That's right. And you are?"

"I'm Mrs. Purdy. Purdy's Mercantile."

"Word travels fast." According to Maxwell, if a miner sneezed at the bottom of the Money Creek Mine, Mrs. Purdy would hear it and have a cold remedy wrapped up and waiting at the store before his drilling mate could say, "Bless you."

"Come to the store with me, and we'll see what you have. I'll tell you up front I drive a hard bargain, and I only buy the best." The woman turned and marched up the street. She didn't even look over her shoulder.

Maggie shrugged and hoisted her case once more. Maxwell was going to pay for this.

A bell jangled as they entered the store. Myriad items from pharmaceuticals to canned goods lined the shelves in military precision, as if they didn't dare be slovenly in the Purdy presence. Mrs. Purdy propped the door open to catch the breeze and hurried around to stand behind the counter. "You can open your case here."

Maggie complied, unbuckling the latches and sending up a prayer of thanks for the loan of Lily's irons this morning.

Mrs. Purdy handled every item in the case, sniffed, peered,

stretched, and otherwise finecombed the merchandise. She scratched figures on a piece of butcher paper, haggled a bit on price, and finally gave Maggie a sizable order.

Maggie withdrew an order slip from the top of the case and filled in the blanks, wondering what Maxwell would say when she informed him she now needed ten chemises and two dozen pairs of lawn drawers with eyelet edging.

While she wrote, Mrs. Purdy talked. "I hear you're staying over to Lily McConnell's place."

"That's right."

The shopkeeper blew a disapproving breath down her sharp nose. "You'd do better to stay at the boardinghouse. Most of this town seems to think the McConnell boys have changed since their wild days, but I don't. Just because Alec married money and Trace got a job as a marshal doesn't mean they've changed. Just means they've overreached themselves. Look at their father. Drunk from morning until night more days than not. The apple doesn't fall far from the tree, I always say, and those apples are rotten fruit from a rotten tree."

Maggie didn't want to appear disloyal to Trace and Lily, but she couldn't resist asking, "Wild days?"

"That's right. Those boys were wilder than Texas long-horns. Always causing trouble, stealing, breaking things. There wasn't a business or residence they didn't hit. Not more than five years ago, all three of them sat in Powers's jail. They had the gall to steal from *me*." She thumped her chest with her index finger, her eyebrows raised, inviting Maggie to be as appalled as she was.

"Five years ago." Maggie did a quick calculation. Cal would've been about eighteen or nineteen and Trace nineteen or twenty. "Have they been involved in stealing since?" Disappointment coursed through her, though she couldn't think why. Cal was nothing to her, and yet, she felt he'd somehow let her down.

Mrs. Purdy twitched. She leaned over the counter and licked her lips. "Nobody can prove it, but I suspect they might have something to do with all the silver that's been stolen off the stage."

Maggie's mouth went dry. Had she hit the mother lode her first day on the case? "What makes you say that?"

Mrs. Purdy raised one finger. "I've been watching. Last year, cattle were going missing around here. The Cross B where all the McConnell boys were working was the worst hit. Who do you think outsmarted the rustlers and broke up the operation? Alec McConnell and his brothers. Colonel Bainbridge was so grateful he handed over his daughter as a reward. And the heir to that big ranch and the stage line and all his business holdings."

She raised another finger. "Then, late last summer, babies and children were being stolen away from their families and sold to who knows where. One was even stolen right out of her dying mother's arms here in Money Creek. And who rides to the rescue? Trace and Cal McConnell. They get the kids back, and Trace McConnell gets a job as a U.S. marshal."

A third finger joined the first two as she counted. "And now, Cal McConnell has gotten himself a job driving stage on a line that's been plagued by robberies. I say it's too convenient and awfully suspicious. Those boys are always around when something goes missing, and they've so far found a way to turn all this misfortune to their advantage. I think they've been in on it all from the very beginning. When it suits them, they turn on their fellow outlaws and take the glory. Wouldn't surprise me a bit if Cal McConnell didn't bring those stage robbers to justice one day and walk away with the reward and everyone calling him a hero. But I'd know better."

The bell jangled and Georgia entered. Her apron today

was yellow with black roosters parading across it. Her hair seemed to be fighting to get out of the bun on the top of her head. She spied Maggie and nodded.

Mrs. Purdy's mouth tightened. "Help you?"

"I just need some salt. I was expecting some on the freight wagon this morning, but my order was short."

Maggie began repacking the case. "I'll be sure to place your order, Mrs. Purdy. You can expect delivery in about two weeks."

"Fine, and you mind what I said about those McConnells." Mrs. Purdy snatched a bag of salt off the shelf behind her and all but tossed it to Georgia. "Some folks around here might treat them like regular folks and better, but I'm not one of them."

Georgia dug in her apron pocket and produced a coin, glaring things unlawful to be uttered, while Maggie continued to pack her bag. They left the store together.

Once out on the boardwalk, Georgia put her hand on Maggie's arm. "Most times I don't interfere in anyone's business, but you're new here, so I'll give you a piece of advice. Don't take as gospel everything Mrs. Purdy says, especially when it comes to the McConnell boys. They once did her a wrong, I'm not denying that, but she holds a grudge longer than anyone I know. Her sour disposition where those boys are concerned could curdle fresh milk."

Maggie nodded. Georgia wasn't exactly an unbiased source when it came to the McConnell boys herself. She was so sweet on Cal she'd make any excuse for him.

Maggie had been in that position herself once before, blinded by love and willing to believe in a man's innocence, even when all the evidence pointed to his guilt. Sadly, she had a feeling time would bring wisdom to Georgia as well.

five

Cal propped his boots on the pile of mailbags in Joe's office and laced his fingers behind his head. "Elko stage is late." He ignored the unease buzzing around his chest. Not every late stage meant another holdup. "You think we'll be ready for daily service to Silver City any time soon? This twice a week gambit has the mail stacking up."

Joe barely glanced up from filling out labels and shrugged. "Dunno. That's a question for the big bosses. I'm just a little tadpole in the company pond. If they want more stages to run, I'm going to need some help around here." He waved to the piles of paper. "They might yank you off the line and stick you behind this counter, like the colonel did when I was down sick with the grippe."

"No, thank you. I'm no hand with ledgers. Two weeks of your job was enough for me." A shout from up the street caught Cal's attention. His boots hit the floor, and he rose to look out the open door. Joe rounded the counter to stand at his shoulder.

A single horse trotted up the main street, a man lying over its neck. Not a saddle horse. Harness flopped and jangled, and the horse sidled and snorted, white showing around its eyes. The familiar star of white on the horse's near-black face made Cal's gut clench. Bennie, the off-wheeler on Farley's team, the team that should be pulling the Elko stage.

The horse skittered to a halt in front of the express office and tossed his head. Farley slid to the ground, blood and dirt covering the side of his face.

Cal dodged the horse and knelt beside the injured man.

"What happened? How bad are you hurt?" He turned on his knees and shouted to Joe. "Get Doc." Cal whipped the kerchief from around his neck and dabbed at the still-oozing gash on Farley's head.

"Got robbed. Same crew." Farley whispered through swollen lips. "Shot Henry. Hit me with a rifle butt."

"Is Henry dead?" Cal blinked. Henry Billington had been the messenger often on Cal's stage runs.

"Yes." Farley closed his eyes and sighed.

"Move over." The doctor elbowed Cal aside and set his bag on the ground. Angus tottered from the livery stable up the street, shading his eyes against the noontime sun, and grabbed the reins of the stage horse that sidled at the corral gate.

Georgia emerged from the café with Maggie on her heels toting her sample case. The sight of Maggie's dark hair and piercing blue eyes sent Cal's heart galloping around his chest. He'd gone to sleep thinking about her and woke up with her still on his mind. Prickly as a chestnut hull but pretty as a sunrise.

A small crowd gathered. The doctor worked quickly then called for assistance.

Cal helped transfer Farley to a blanket to carry him to the doctor's place.

They had just turned into the gate in front of the doctor's house when Powers strode up. "What happened?"

"Stage got robbed south of here. At least one dead and the driver hurt." Tiredness and frustration weighed on Cal's shoulders. He helped get Farley into the house then returned to the front porch where Powers was addressing the knot of people at the gate.

Georgia had her arms crossed and a stormy look in her eye. Maggie stood at Georgia's elbow. She tugged at her lower lip, and a crease formed between her brows.

"My deputies and I will look into this."

"I'm going with you." Cal took his gun from its holster and checked the chambers, bracing himself for an argument.

"I'll have plenty of manpower without you." Powers didn't even look at Cal. "Jack, you and Kane swing by Purdy's and pick up a couple more boxes of cartridges."

"Powers, I'm going. If not as a member of the posse then as a representative of the stage company. I'll go and recover the company's property."

The glare Powers turned on Cal was hot enough to start a fire. "Fine, but you'll follow orders, or I'll arrest you for obstructing justice. You're too used to running maverick around here. I won't have a man who can't take orders on my posse."

Cal rode out with the posse an hour later. Ten men, loaded for bear, trailing in Powers's wake. Farley hadn't regained consciousness, so all they knew was that the shotgun messenger had been killed.

Though he knew each of the men in the posse, Cal said nothing. Hecker, as one of the shareholders in the stage line, had backed Cal, insisting the sheriff allow a company representative along. Powers had said nothing to Cal since. Which was just how Cal liked it.

They rode for almost an hour before Cal smelled it. Smoke. A whiff at first, then stronger. The posse rounded an outcropping of rock, and the charred remains of a Concord stagecoach appeared on the road below them. Everyone pulled up, and Cal nudged his horse forward to get a better view.

Powers laid the side of his rifle barrel against Cal's chest. "Hold up, McConnell. The law goes first. You wait here. We'll let you know when you can come down, though from the looks of things, you wasted a trip. Doesn't look like there's much company property to recover."

The gloating in his voice grated on Cal. The sheriff's petty triumphs knew no bounds. He'd use any excuse to score off a McConnell, and Cal in particular. Having no choice, Cal waited on the ridge above while the rest of the men fanned out. Finally, Powers signaled with a wave that Cal could approach.

The smoke smell lingered over the blackened wood and metal that had once been a stagecoach. Cal dismounted and stripped a branch off a scrub bush nearby to poke through the rubble. The leather bottom of a mailbag, a pocketknife, and the chased silver handle of Farley's bull-hide whip. No bodies. Of that he was thankful, but where were they? Had the stage been empty except for the mail and the express box? And where was the express box?

Jack, one of the deputies, knelt in the brush a few yards off the trail, his head and shoulders showing above the scrub.

"You got something?" Cal approached the young deputy.

"Uh-huh." The express box lay open to the sunshine and empty as a miser's heart. Near the box, Henry Billington lay sprawled, a single gunshot to his chest. Jack shook his head. "I've known Henry for a long time. Always ready to lend a hand." He rubbed his hand across his jaw. "This is getting outright scary. First time they've burned the stage."

"Any sign of the horses?"

"Not yet, but I haven't left this area. Some of the others might come across them. Powers had them fan out to look for passengers."

Cal went to his horse and untied the slicker behind the cantle of his saddle. He returned and spread it over Henry. "I'm going to scout around."

"Cal?"

He turned.

Jack stood, cradling his rifle at his waist. "I just wanted you to know I don't approve of the way Powers treats you. You've always been square with me, and I've got no quarrel with you."

Cal nodded. "Good to know, Jack. Thanks." He returned to the burned-out stage carcass. A stagecoach wasn't all that easy to torch. Had they brought kerosene along with them, or had they improvised? Gunpowder perhaps?

He gave up trying to recreate the crime and turned his attention to studying the tracks surrounding the coach instead. Some boot prints and several different horse tracks. Cal gritted his teeth. If Powers had allowed Cal to go in first instead of letting his entire posse run all over the site, maybe Cal would have been able to find something helpful.

He moved off the trail. At least two robbers, he figured. Farley and Henry probably wouldn't have stopped for one man. They'd have fired on a lone gunman and whipped up the team. That's what Cal would've done. Behind a large rock, big enough to conceal a man on horseback, he found fresh horse droppings. At least one of them had waited here.

Cal followed the tracks for perhaps thirty yards where the single tracks joined several others, and then he squatted to study the marks in the sandy dirt. One caught his eye. He knew that track. He'd followed it before. The horse that made this track was a shaggy, black-and-white pinto that toed out and overreached his off-hind.

Cal's blood boiled at the thought of his rider. Hack. A man responsible for at least one other stage robbery, one that Cal's sister-in-law, Clara, had been a passenger on. One of the men responsible for the kidnapping of Cal's niece, Rose, last fall.

Trace and Cal had searched for Hack for months but come up empty.

Don't jump to conclusions. Maybe it isn't him. All you know is that it's his pinto.

And yet, how far of a stretch was it to assume Hack had returned to his stage-robbing ways?

"What are you doing over here?" Powers rounded the

boulder and rode his horse smack over the tracks. "Did you find anything?"

Cal straightened. "Any sign of the passengers?"

"Get back over by the stage with Jack and don't go poking around. For all I know you could be destroying evidence."

Cal envisioned pushing his fist through Powers's face then had to ask a quick prayer for forgiveness. He took his time returning to the stage, and Powers followed, letting his mount breathe down Cal's neck with every step.

Cal stopped to contemplate the scene once more. "You didn't answer my question. Did you find any passengers?"

The sheriff grunted. "Two men. Shot. Looks like they were running away from the coach. Both hit in the back."

"Any sign of the horses?"

"We found three, all still in harness but cut loose from each other. Kane's bringing them in. Haven't found the other two horses yet, but I imagine they'll turn up."

"Three dead, one wounded, horses missing, cashbox empty, and the coach burned to cinders."

"That about sums it up."

"This one feels different. They've never shot the passengers before, and they've never burned the stage."

They reached Jack. Powers pulled up and crossed his wrists on his saddle horn. "You didn't answer my question either."

Cal pushed back his hat and hooked his thumbs into his belt loops before he looked up at Powers. "What question?"

"I asked if you found anything." Powers swept his hand toward the burned-out shell.

"Nope. Not a thing." He shrugged off the prick his conscience gave him. After all, what did he really know? Best to wait and tell Trace about the tracks. That way Cal couldn't be accused of sending Powers out on a wild-goose chase.

❧

Maggie chafed waiting for the posse to return. If only she'd been able to come up with a plausible reason to accompany the sheriff. Her investigation was hampered by being on her own. If Maxwell or Trace had been here, they would've gone along as a matter of course.

She sat at a table in the café where she could watch down the Elko road and leafed through a week-old paper. What had happened out there, and how could she find out? She sent up a prayer that God would protect the posse and that perhaps they'd capture the robbers. *You can work it out, Lord. Nothing's too hard for You. Keep them safe.* All *of them.*

"You staring down that road won't make them return any quicker." Georgia settled into a chair across from her. "You done not reading that paper?"

Maggie folded the pages and set them beside her plate. "I guess I'm a little edgy. Have you heard anything more about the injured man?"

"Yes." Georgia's chair creaked. "I took some broth down there a while ago for the patient, and a pot roast and pie for the doc. He's a bachelor, and he forgets to eat unless someone reminds him."

"What did the doctor say about the driver?"

"Farley's got a hard head, that's for sure. Doc put a dozen stitches in his forehead and said Farley was babbling and inco. . .inco. . ." She stopped.

"Incoherent?"

"That was the word. I guess my lack of book learning is showing. Doc uses two-dollar words where a ten-cent one would do."

"Doctors are like that." Maggie picked up her cup and covered her smile. Not for worlds would she hurt the feelings of this generous woman.

"You waiting for that posse for a particular reason?"

The question made Maggie instantly wary. "No particular reason. Why?"

Georgia picked up a fork from the place setting before her and polished it with the edge of her apron. "You being so new in town, I wouldn't figure you'd know anyone who rode out well enough to be anxious about their return." She paused. "Unless it would be Cal."

"Cal? Why would I be waiting for Cal to return?"

She shrugged. "I thought maybe you might be getting sweet on him. You wouldn't be the first. I'd venture to say every unmarried girl in this town, and probably a few of the married ones, too, have had romantic ideas about Cal at one time or another."

"I suspected he was some sort of local Lothario." Disgust and disappointment settled around Maggie's heart.

"Lo-what?"

"Lothario. A man who chases girls and toys with their affections. Lothario was a character in a play."

Georgia snorted. "You didn't hear me. I said girls had set their caps for Cal. I didn't say he chased after those girls."

Maggie lowered her chin and widened her eyes. "He's not a flirt?"

A chuckle made Georgia's apron bounce. "Naw, he's just nice to people. Sometimes girls get the wrong idea because he keeps things light and easy. You wouldn't know it from the way he acts, but Cal's seen some pretty dark times."

Maggie told herself that her interest was merely professional, a chance to gain more insight into a possible suspect, not because anything about Cal McConnell attracted her. Mrs. Purdy had mentioned his run-ins with the law.

"What sort of dark times? You mean because of his father?"

"That's part of it. A big part. Angus McConnell never was much of a father to his sons, but when Cal was a youngster, his mother and little sister died. He and his brothers ran wild. Breaking things, getting into fights, terrorizing folks with their antics. Cal even rode his horse into the church one Sunday morning. Eventually, all three boys landed in jail for stealing, but the lady they stole from, instead of pressing charges, took them home to her ranch. It took some doing, but eventually every one of those boys turned his life around. They're all fine, upstanding, God-fearing men who would do anything for you. Alec's a ranch foreman, Trace is a lawman, and Cal drives stage."

Maggie mulled this information. Could a man really change that much? Her experience told her once a scoundrel always a scoundrel, and it was the ones who pretended to change that needed watching the most.

Georgia continued. "I surmise that Cal likes to keep things light because he's found that if he lets people get too close, they can hurt him. Like his ma dying, like his pa being a drunk. Cal is everybody's friend, but nobody's close friend. Unless it's one of his brothers. The bond those boys share is something special. Me and Clara and Lily have talked of it a few times. They're all waiting for Cal to fall hard for someone. Clara thinks when the right girl comes into his life, he'll forget about the possibility of getting hurt. He'll think the risk is worth it. I just hope whoever she is, she's the kind of girl who will be worthy of him, someone who won't let him down."

Did Georgia long to be that woman? The café owner had to be ten years older than Cal. Maggie touched her necklace, threading the long, flat links through her fingers. Why should the thought of Georgia and Cal bother her?

"I've never seen a necklace like that one." Georgia inclined her head toward Maggie.

She let the links drop back onto her white blouse. The sound of hooves on the hard road caught her attention. She leaned to get a better view up the street. "They're back."

The posse rode in slowly, leading several of the stage

horses, and across three of them lay canvas-covered bodies. There was no sign of the coach.

Cal led one of the horses, and when Maggie and Georgia went onto the café porch to watch the procession, he looked right into Maggie's eyes. A shiver went through her at the determined, hard expression she saw there. Then the corner of his mouth quirked up, and he touched his hat brim. The harsh lines and determined set to his jaw melted away, and like the sun coming out, he grinned, though whether his smile was aimed at her or at Georgia, Maggie couldn't tell.

six

After a bumpy day's ride on the stage, Maggie gathered her belongings and prepared to disembark in the hillside mining community of Silver City.

Cal wrenched the door open before she could reach for the latch and held up his hand to help her from the coach. He kept possession of her hand, squeezing her fingers until she looked up at him. "Silver City is full of rowdy miners, and there's no sheriff here. I wouldn't let Clara or Lily walk around on their own, and I'm not letting you, so you might as well just get used to it and get over your fussing."

"I don't need a keeper." What would he say if he knew she carried a gun and knew how to use it?

"I don't want to have to go home and tell Lily I let you get harmed. For some reason, she's taken quite a shine to you."

"You don't have to sound so surprised."

He shrugged. "Lily says you're sweet. Guess it goes to show you can be nice when you want to. Wish you wanted to more often with me. I get tired of the cactus spines you grow every time I get near."

She chewed her lower lip. Truth was her snippy attitude tired her as well. It was just that she couldn't trust him. . . or any other man. Down that road lay heartbreak and humiliation.

He carried her bags into the hotel and made a thorough check of her room before handing her the key. "The hotel always keeps a bed here at the end of the hall for the stage driver." He pointed to a cot under the window two doors down. "So I'll be close in case you need something."

She accepted the key and his offer to escort her to dinner, but she made sure she paid her own way. Being polite didn't mean she would be beholden to a man.

For the next two days as she wandered from store to store and into the bank and stage office, he remained true to his word, never letting her out of his sight. Agent Maggie Davis bristled at his being underfoot and hampering her sleuthing, but lonely woman Maggie Davis appreciated his chivalry. Each side thought the other daft.

By the time they arrived back in Money Creek, Maggie felt more comfortable with Cal but had made almost no headway on the case. Questioning the bank manager and the ticket agent as she had in Money Creek hadn't turned up any new leads in Silver City. About the only thing she had to show for herself were several more orders for petticoats and corset covers.

They made two more trips between the mining towns over the next ten days. The hours spent inside the rocking stagecoach gave her time to mull over Georgia's story of Cal's past and to begin to see beyond the surface facets of his character. Cal might have more substance than first appeared. He certainly took his job seriously. His care of his team and equipment reassured her. He could be diligent when he wanted to be. And his behavior toward her was exemplary.

They passed now-familiar buildings arriving at Money Creek. The stage pulled in under a red, white, and blue bunting being erected across Main Street. Mrs. Purdy stood in the middle of the road, her fists jammed on her bombazine hips, yelling at the two men on ladders. "No, Jake, higher on your side. Kane, stop yanking it. If you tear that fabric after all the trouble I had getting it gathered evenly, I'll have your hide nailed to the barn door before supper."

Maggie allowed Cal to lift her from the coach. His hands spanned her waist, and he held her a moment after her feet hit the boardwalk. To settle her oddly fluttering heart, she asked him, "What's the bunting for?"

"Tomorrow's the Fourth, remember?" He grinned. "It's a cowboy's duty to celebrate the Fourth of July." He swept off his hat and held it to his chest.

"You're not a cowboy."

"I have been, in my younger days."

"Riding a stick horse and firing a peashooter doesn't make you a cowboy."

He dropped his jaw and reeled back in mock pain. "I'll have you know I've herded cattle, branded cattle, driven cattle, delivered their calves, and all but rocked the little darlin's to sleep. If that doesn't qualify me as a cowboy, then I don't know what does."

He resettled his hat. "C'mon. I'll walk you over to Lily's." He took her bags. "I don't want to get into an argument with Mrs. Purdy. The party out at the ranch is a bone of contention for her. Soon as she heard they were having one, she started planning one for the town. Now folks don't know what to do, accept the colonel's hospitality or Mrs. Purdy's. Colonel Bainbridge invited her to the ranch, but she'd rather step in cow dung than set foot on the Cross B."

A hollow feeling settled into the pit of her stomach. A party at the Cross B ranch and a party in Money Creek, and she hadn't been invited to either. Because she didn't fit in. She was a stranger, a nomad who would fade out of their lives as soon as her job ended.

Maggie had a strange sense of comfort entering the house. It felt familiar, like home. She hadn't had a home in a very long time. Since her father passed away, it had been a series of boardinghouses and hotels, always working, always moving. Staying with Lily was different. Lily treated Maggie like a sister. Maggie's secrecy about her real work weighed heavier on her mind with each passing day—something that had never happened to her before—though she refused to examine why now should be different.

Rose toddled across the floor to greet them, and instead of throwing herself against Cal's legs, as was her custom, she came right to Maggie and lifted her arms. "Up." The baby's first word, exclaimed over and praised a week before, now came at ever-increasing intervals.

Maggie swallowed. To this point, she'd managed to avoid holding the baby.

"Up." Rose increased the volume, as if the only reason she wasn't obeyed instantly was because Maggie hadn't heard her.

"She'll just get louder. You might as well pick her up." Cal set her cases at the base of the stairs and hung his hat on a peg.

Uncertain, Maggie put her hands under Rose's arms and lifted her onto her hip like she'd seen Lily do. The little girl grinned. She smelled of talcum and milk and sunshine.

Lily stood in the kitchen door wiping her hands on her apron. "Welcome home, you two. I'm glad you made it in time for supper."

Cal sniffed the air like a hound. "Ham and potatoes? That's my favorite."

Lily rolled her eyes. "It's chicken and rice."

He grinned. "That's my favorite, too."

Maggie followed them into the kitchen with Rose, reluctant to put the girl down now that she'd mustered courage enough to hold her. A wave of heat hit her when Lily opened the oven door.

"Did you ask her yet?" Lily turned from the stove, gripping a hot pan with a tea towel. She served up three plates of steaming food. "It's too hot in here. Let's go to the back porch. Rose has had her supper, so she can play while we eat. I'll carry yours, Maggie. Cal, bring the rest, will you?" She took two plates and used her hip to open the screen door.

"Ask me what?" Maggie followed Cal outside. Lily sat in

one of the rockers, and Maggie took the other, easing Rose down to stand on the porch.

Cal took his plate and sat on the steps, bracing his back against the railing. "She's been so prickly toward me, I was thinking of having you ask her, Lily, but since she's decided to start playing nice this week, I'll give it a shot." He grinned at Maggie. "Tomorrow morning, early, we're headed to the Cross B to celebrate the Fourth. We'd sure like it if you would come with us."

The inviting expression in Cal's eyes warmed Maggie through. Before she could talk herself out of it, she accepted. "I'd be happy to come. Thank you."

When Cal rose and took their empty plates back into the kitchen, he put his hand on Maggie's shoulder and gave it a squeeze on the way by.

꙳

Cal wasn't joshing when he said they would leave early. In the pre-dawn gloom, Maggie helped Lily load the wagon with baked goods and overnight bags. Cal made a nest for the sleeping Rose in one corner of the wagon box. Lily opted to ride in the back with Rose, leaving Maggie to sit beside Cal.

Maggie couldn't quit yawning. Lying awake most of the night sorting out the precious few leads she had on the case as well as reminding herself why she should keep her distance from Cal made her extra sleepy and dull this morning. That Cal seemed to be as cheerful and bright as ever set her teeth on edge.

He stopped the wagon in front of the Rusty Bucket and hopped down. "I'll go get Georgia." When Maggie made to move into the back, he shook his head. "No, she'll ride in the back with Lily. You stay where you are."

In a moment, he returned holding a basket of food. Georgia locked the door and came out tying her enormous sunbonnet. A thin, old man with sallow skin and rheumy eyes tottered after her carrying a bedroll and a valise.

"Maggie, this is Angus." Cal plunked the basket into the wagon.

She looked from Cal to Angus.

Lily answered Maggie's unspoken question. "Angus is Cal's father, my father-in-law. Good morning, Angus."

Maggie saw no resemblance. Dark-haired and gaunt, Angus McConnell looked used up enough to be Cal's grandfather. His clothes hung on him, and his bones almost poked through his skin.

Cal slid a plank through braces on either side of the wagon to form a seat. Georgia used the high boardwalk to assist herself over the side and onto the plank. Angus climbed up and sat in the back, his feet hanging over the tailgate. Lily settled herself next to Georgia, within easy reach of Rose who slumbered away. Lucky baby. Another yawn threatened to split Maggie's jaw.

Sunrise slipped over the town as Cal drove the team south toward the Cross B. The trip to the ranch took them through some of the most beautiful scenery Maggie had encountered. Tall bluffs towered up from the valley floor, and the waters of Money Creek chuckled and scurried over rocks.

Maggie perked up when Georgia unpacked a flask of coffee and some fresh bread and butter. Lily and Georgia talked together and played with Rose, who had awakened as cheerful as her uncle Cal.

Maggie popped the last bit of her bread into her mouth. She washed the yeasty-buttery taste down with coffee, careful not to spill it as the wagon lurched along. "So, your brother and his wife live at the Cross B?"

He nodded. "Alec's the foreman. Colonel Bainbridge owns the ranch, and Alec is married to his daughter." Cal slapped the reins and chirruped to the horses.

"I've heard the colonel's name in town."

"He and his wife took us boys in and gave us jobs a few years ago. That's where I learned to punch cows." He shrugged. "I liked it well enough, but Alec was the one who really took to it. The colonel made him foreman just about the same time Mrs. Bainbridge died. We owe a lot to the Bainbridges. If it wasn't for them, us McConnells would most likely all be in the territorial prison or dead. We were sure headed that way."

Maggie looked back where Angus had one arm slung over the side and lurched with the movement of the wagon. "What about Angus?"

Cal pressed his lips together. "He couldn't stay out of a bottle long enough to raise three boys after my ma died. So we did it ourselves, and we were making a pretty poor job of it when Mrs. Bainbridge bailed us out of jail and brought us to the ranch. We got a whole new life then. Learned what it meant to work hard. The colonel worked us from dawn till dark." He chuckled. "Sometimes I think he gave us so much work to do so we wouldn't have time to get into trouble. Mrs. Bainbridge treated us like we were her own sons. Loved us and scolded us and taught us how to treat women. Both of them taught us how much we needed God's love and forgiveness."

"The colonel sounds a little like my father. He taught me about God and work from the cradle up. I used to help him in his shop." She touched her necklace.

"What kind of shop?"

"He was a locksmith. He made locks and keys and combination safes." She hadn't spoken to anyone about her father in a long time. "He passed away a few years ago."

Cal nodded and cleared his throat. "There's the ranch." He pulled up for a moment on a rise. Below them on the left, Money Creek lay like a discarded silver ribbon on the valley floor, and ahead in a hollow surrounded by canyon walls, a fine ranch house, an enormous barn, and what seemed like miles of corral fence marked the headquarters of the Cross B.

"What a beautiful setting." The walls rose in pink, gray, and yellow layers, catching the sunlight. Maggie lifted her curly bangs off her forehead to allow the breeze to cool her skin. The day was already warming up, and by afternoon it would be scorching.

As they drove in, signs of the celebration to come became apparent. Several cowboys hung streamers and lanterns and erected sawhorses and planks to serve as tables. Between the house and the barn, two cowboys drove metal poles into the ground over a fire pit.

"They'll be roasting a steer on that spit most of the day." Cal stopped the wagon in front of the house and leaped down. He reached up for Maggie's waist and swung her to the ground.

"Cal, Lily, you made it." A pretty blue-eyed woman came out the front door holding a bowl on her hip. Her apron stretched across her middle, proclaiming her clearly in the family way. "And Georgia and Angus. Welcome."

"Clara, this is Maggie Davis." Cal took Maggie's elbow and led her to the porch. "She's boarding with Lily. Maggie, this is Clara, my brother's wife."

Maggie nodded to Clara. "Thank you for having me. I hope it isn't an imposition."

"Not at all. We're delighted." Clara handed the bowl to Cal and wiped her hands on her apron. "Rose, sweetheart, look how you've grown." She went to the wagon and reached up for the baby so Lily could climb down. "You're getting so big."

Georgia started emptying the wagon. "Where do you want this food, Clara?"

A tall, dark-haired cowboy emerged from the barn, his long strides easily eating up the distance between the barn and the house. Something about his jawline and the effortless way he walked caught Maggie's attention.

"Maggie, this is my brother, Alec. Alec, Maggie Davis." Cal set the bowl on the top step and took a basket from Georgia's hands.

His brother, of course. Brown eyes the same shape as Cal's blue ones studied Maggie. She smiled and held out her hand. He gave it a quick shake then turned to his wife. His entire expression changed, softening, and his eyes took on a gleam. "Here, give me that girl. She's too heavy for you to be toting around in your delicate condition." He reached for Rose and settled her on his forearm. His other arm went around Clara's waist and pulled her into his side. He brushed a kiss across the top of her hair. "I'm thinking we should've skipped the party. This is too much for you."

Maggie turned away from the cozy, family scene. Agents who worked secretly for the U.S. Marshal's office couldn't afford to let anyone that close. Which made Maggie the perfect candidate for this type of work. She didn't trust anyone anyway.

seven

Cal swiped his forehead with his sleeve and took another nail from between his teeth. From the size of the crowd that had been gathering since mid-morning, Money Creek Township must look like a ghost town about now. Poor old Mrs. Purdy.

He hammered the last nail in place and picked up his wood scraps. "There. That's one thing Alec can cross off his list."

"He's as jumpy as a June bug in a skillet getting all the details sorted out." Seb Lewis stepped up onto the corral fence and hooked his arms over the top rail. "Gonna be a fine day for a rodeo."

"Looks like it. You riding?"

"Figured I'd try my hand at the wild horse breaking. And maybe the calf roping. You?"

"Alec's counting on me to compete. Wants to make this rodeo as big as Bill Cody's down in Nebraska. A shame I have to ride today though. I brought some feminine company along with me from town. Might be fun to sit on the stands between two nice girls and watch the rest of you get your heads busted."

Seb fingered the button on his cuff. "Saw you came with Georgia and that Davis girl. You sparking her?"

"Georgia or Maggie Davis?" Cal bit the inside of his cheek. "They're both mighty fine women. A fellow could go farther and fare worse, I figure. Maybe you should try your hand at sparking."

The tough rancher rubbed his jaw and wrinkled his nose. "No, thank you. I'll take my chances with the horses. Less likely to end up with broken bones thataway."

"There's something to that." Cal smiled. "But don't forget, the winner of each event gets first choice of a dance partner tonight. That's something worth fighting for, isn't it?"

"Fellow like you doesn't need that kind of advantage," Seb said, replacing his hat. "You already have girls lining up to dance with you."

Cal flexed his fingers. What Seb said might be true—he'd never lacked for partners at a dance—but would Maggie be one of them? Doubtful. Though she'd thawed a little toward him, he still had the feeling she was holding something back, still skittish. Wariness clouded her eyes, like she carried a still-tender wound. It made him want to soothe the hurt, to make her forget to be guarded. He wanted to know the real Maggie Davis, the one who hid behind that touch-me-not expression.

And he'd caught glimpses of the real her, even today. When she'd tipped her face up to the rising sun this morning and breathed deep of the dawn air. When his sisters-in-law had led her into the house like she was family, and the confused, pleased look on her face. She'd bloomed like a flower, laughing and easy like he hadn't seen before. He wished she could be that easy with him. Somehow, whenever he was with her, he found himself either tongue-tied or sticking his foot into his mouth all the way to his knee and making her mad.

Seb grinned. "You look like a moonstruck bull calf. Guess I know what girl you'll be asking."

"Maybe." Cal hopped down. "Have to see. Anyway, I might not win. If you win, you'll have to ask someone to dance. You got anyone in mind?"

The rancher studied the picnic area by the house. "The horse I drew is called Dervish. That black with the white socks. Alec found him running lose on the Lazy P. He's got a mean look in his eye, kinda like the gal I'm thinking of asking to dance." He rolled his thin shoulders and joined Cal on the ground.

"I got a dun named Cougar. You know him?"

Seb grinned. "I surely do. I own him. Been keeping him special for today. Alec was glad to hear I had some rough stock to add to the pen. He put the word out to more than a dozen ranches looking for their rankest stock. Cougar jumps like he's got a bellyful of bedsprings."

His gleeful expression made Cal chuckle. "You don't need to look so happy. You'll probably win in a runaway, and the rest of us will be too stove up to dance anyway." A movement from near the barn caught his eye. He waved back at Alec, who beckoned.

"Is he riding today?"

"Nope. He says he's got enough to do this year just organizing stuff." With a grunt, Cal tested the strength of the chute then pitched the last loose scrap into a bucket. He sniffed the tangy air blowing from the direction of the fire pit. "Hope whatever Alec wants doesn't take long. I'm so hungry my stomach thinks my throat's been cut."

"Looks like Sheriff Powers there with your brother." Seb frowned. "I guess I'll mosey over to the picnic tables. Powers and I get along about as well as barbed wire and bare skin."

Cal took a deep breath and cinched up his self-control before crossing the open ground. "Sheriff." He set the bucket of scraps down and stuck his hammer in amongst the lumber. "Alec, the chutes are ready."

"Good. Right after lunch you can help me move the calves into the holding pen." Alec dug in his shirt pocket and withdrew a piece of crumpled paper and a stubby pencil. He licked the point and made a couple of notes. Without looking up, he said, "Sheriff wanted a word with you."

Cal faced Powers. Seb had it right. The local sheriff had all the charm of a coil of barbed wire. "Surprised to see you here today, Sheriff. Thought you'd be at the town celebration."

Belligerence sat heavy on Powers's face. "I would be if I didn't think I was needed out here more. This rodeo has brought in all the rabble in the territory. I'm here to keep an eye on things." His glare left no doubt that he considered Cal part of that rabble.

"And here I thought you came for the dinner and dance." Cal kept his voice as bland as cream.

The sheriff tucked his thumbs into his belt just under his paunch. Dusky color started near his collar and ran up into his face, and his eyes narrowed to slits. "I talked to Hecker over to the bank. He seems to think you should be extra careful these next few runs to Silver City. Nervous as a long-tailed cat in a room full of rocking chairs."

Cal's attention sharpened. "He say why?"

"Nope."

"What about putting a deputy on the stage?"

"I can't spare a man on the off chance something *might* happen. It's up to the stage company to provide security." Powers thrust his thick finger toward Cal. "That means it's on you." His eyebrow quirked and his lips formed a sneer. "Though that's like trusting a wolf with a lamb. I tried to warn Hecker, but he wasn't having any." He turned on his heel and strode away.

Alec stuffed his list back into his pocket and clapped Cal on the shoulder. "His manners get worse every day. He mostly leaves Trace and me alone now, but he's forever digging his spurs into you. Maybe I should have a word with the colonel about him."

Cal shook his head. "Don't bother. I can deal with Powers."

"Maybe, but you watch your back, little brother. He's got a lot of venom stored up where you're concerned. I'd hate to see you get snakebit."

"He's more rattle than strike. Let's go get some of that good food I've been smelling before he gets it all." Cal smiled, though he took Alec's concerns to heart. Powers did have it in for him, and he'd be wise to step carefully where the sheriff was concerned. "I've got a hankering for pie."

"When don't you?" Alec smacked his shoulder again and headed for the picnic area.

❧

Maggie spent an hour bent over the washtub, up to her elbows in sudsy water. Lily seemed to have boundless energy, clearing tables, carrying dishes, and drying plates as fast as Maggie could wash them. When the last dish towel hung on the line behind the house, the women sank down around a picnic table in the shade with glasses of apple juice, thankful to get off their feet.

"The rodeo is starting in a bit." Georgia laid her cool glass against her temple.

Maggie rested her elbow on the table and propped her chin on the heel of her hand. Her back ached, and her sleepless night dragged at her eyelids. Rose napped on a blanket in the shade of the house, and Maggie had half a mind to join the little girl.

Cal and Seb approached, and Maggie straightened up, lethargy fleeing.

Seb swept his hat off, revealing iron gray locks. "You ladies coming over to watch? Us cowboys need a cheering section, you know."

"And bandages for the inevitable?" Clara levered herself up, and Cal put his arm under her elbow to help her.

"That, too." His dimple flashed. "Me and Seb might need a little gentle treatment after we ride. Alec's rounded up a rank bunch of horses for us this year."

"Seb? You're riding?" Georgia snorted and glared at the older cowboy. "Foolish thing to do at your age." She clambered to her feet. "I'll come, and I'll be rooting for you, Cal."

Maggie glanced from Cal to Georgia. Cal might think it only friendly banter between him and Georgia, but Maggie wasn't so certain. Georgia sure put a lot of feeling into her words. Maggie hoped Georgia wasn't in for heartache.

She found herself between Lily and Georgia on the top tier of the makeshift stands. The sunshine beat down, nearly blinding her and making her grateful for the shade her straw hat provided.

Georgia wore a heavily ruffled calico sunbonnet that stuck out past her face and kept her fair skin covered. It also served as a bit of a megaphone for her voice. She cheered enthusiastically for most of the cowboys, though loudest for Cal and not at all for Seb. "Stupid fool ought to know better." When Seb won the calf roping, she crossed her arms and sniffed.

Cal seemed to be everywhere behind the chutes, helping load horses and cattle. He and Seb competed together in the team roping and finished second. A man Maggie recognized as the town blacksmith had assumed the duties of announcer. He shouted out the last event of the day: wild horse breaking.

As the riders each took a turn trying to stick on the backs of unbroken horses, Georgia alternated between throttling her handkerchief and using it to mop her face.

Lily flicked a fan, trying to create a breeze. "I'm glad Clara decided to stay in the house with Rose. It's too hot for either of them out here."

"Cal McConnell on Cougar."

An anxious thrill shot through Maggie. She forced herself to stay still, but everything in her rooted for Cal to win. That wasn't bad, was it? It would be callous not to cheer for him, right?

Cal jumped down from the top rail and headed toward the

center of the corral. A group of cowboys surrounded a horse, hanging on to his halter and getting twisted and jerked around as the animal fought them. Someone slung a saddle over the horse's back and reached underneath the animal's belly to grab the cinch.

With what seemed scant regard for his safety, Cal grabbed a handful of mane and leaped astride.

The men loosened their hold, and the yellow horse exploded in several directions at once with Cal stuck to his back. Cal hung on by his knees and a long rope attached to the horse's halter. His other hand flew in the air above his head, jerking with each impact of the horse's legs on the dirt.

Maggie didn't breathe, pressing her fingers against her lips. Each jarring thud of hooves ricocheted through her, and she clenched her teeth so hard her jaw ached.

An eternity later, the timer struck the cowbell. Cal's hand came down on the saddle horn, and he flipped his leg over the horse's neck and leaped neatly to the ground. When he landed, he swept his hat off and searched the cheering crowd. His eyes stopped moving when he found Maggie's face.

The spectators faded away, and all she could see was the light in his eyes. Her heart beat thick in her ears. She swallowed hard and slowly sat down, becoming aware that she was the only one standing. Heat swirled in her ears when Georgia gave her a speculative look. Lily snickered and patted Maggie's hand.

Cal gave a courtly bow, his smile shooting Maggie through with sparkly arrows, then headed over to the corral gate to help with the next horse.

"Seb Lewis on Dervish."

Maggie tried to calm her heart. She sneaked a peek at Georgia, who dabbed her throat and studied her nails. The same group of cowboys got half dragged into the arena, hanging off a huge, black horse. When Seb mounted, he shot a look into the stands as if searching for someone.

Then the men fell away, and the horse burst into action. The animal rose high on his back legs, his forelegs pawing air. Heavy black mane shrouded Seb. Dervish didn't bother coming down before leaping forward and kicking his back legs so high Maggie feared he'd go over onto his head. On his next jump, he twisted like he was trying to turn himself inside out. His belly flashed, and he crow-hopped. Seb stuck like a thistle.

An uneasy feeling swept over Maggie when Dervish quit bucking and ran, flat out, right at the corral fence in front of the stands. Seb wrenched the horse's head around, but the animal ran on. The little rancher's yell mingled with the cries of the crowd and an eerie scream from Dervish. Spectators on the lower benches scattered. Frozen to her seat, Maggie closed her eyes just before the impact.

A cracking, splintering crash rent the air. Maggie's eyes popped open in time to see Seb slung off and flying over the top rail. He hit the ground with his upper back and somersaulted to a halt in a cloud of dust. The fence held, barely, and Dervish, now rid of his rider, staggered back, gathered himself, and sprinted in the other direction.

Georgia shot up. "Seb! My darling!"

eight

Maggie yanked her feet aside to keep from getting them flattened in Georgia's charge down the row. Dumbstruck, Maggie followed in time to see Georgia lift Seb's hand to her lips. "Sebastian Lewis, you old goat, you'd better not be dead." Her voice, so soft and tender and choked with tears, froze Maggie. Georgia bit back a sob and used her handkerchief to wipe the dirt from his cheek.

While lookers-on milled and murmured, Cal skimmed between the cracked corral boards and knelt beside the prone man. He loosened Seb's collar and leaned in to listen. "His heart's beating and he's breathing."

Maggie caught the relief in his voice, but she couldn't help but stare, trying to ascertain the impact Georgia's declaration might have on Cal. And, if she was honest, the impact it had on herself. She felt exactly as if she had missed a step in the dark.

Lily's mouth hung slightly open, her eyes blinking slowly. "I had no idea. I had *no* idea."

"Excuse me. Pardon me." The doctor who had treated the injured stage driver in town edged through the crowd.

"Doc." Cal moved back to allow him room.

Georgia didn't budge, tears streaking her cheeks, her lips moving in what Maggie could only assume were prayers. Maggie added her own prayer for Seb.

The doctor did a quick check. "Seb, can you hear me?" He thumbed up one of Seb's eyelids.

Seb groaned and swatted at the doctor's hand.

Maggie's sigh of relief mingled with Lily's.

"Ah, got the wind knocked out of you?" The doctor looked into his other eye. "Anything hurt? Anything broken?"

"Naw, Doc, just my pride." He started to sit up, but several hands pushed him back.

An inelegant snort erupted from Georgia.

Seb's eyes widened. "Is that you, Georgia?"

"Oh, Seb darlin', I thought you were dead." She caressed his gnarled hand and rubbed the back of it against her wet cheek.

A faint smile flickered across his face. "I think I am. I think I died and went right to heaven, because I'm looking at an angel this very minute."

What had come over them? Those two bickered and sniped at each other like two dogs with one bone every time Maggie saw them together in the Rusty Bucket, and here they were in front of half of Money Creek billing and cooing like a couple of lovesick dying ducks.

Georgia blushed to her roots.

Seb reached out with his other hand and cupped her cheek. "You did call me your darlin', didn't you? I didn't imagine that."

"No, Seb, you didn't imagine it." Again her soft, almost shy voice surprised Maggie.

He relaxed, smiling, and let his hand fall to his chest. "Then I can die a happy man."

"Die? Are you hurt bad?"

"Naw, you can't hurt a tough old goat like me." His grin widened in his dirt-streaked face. He sat up and pushed aside Cal's helping hand. "I'm fine." He never took his eyes from Georgia's face. "I got everything I need right here to make me feel just dandy." He rose and stood beside her, a good head shorter. "I could use some cider though, and maybe a slice of pie." He winked, and Georgia blushed again. When he offered her his arm, she latched on to it like she thought he might get away, and together they walked toward the house, leaving everyone staring after them.

Alec climbed onto the top rail of the fence and held up his hands. "Folks, that concludes our rodeo. You all take a little time to refresh yourself, enjoy some cider in the shade. There will be a couple of speeches and a reading of the Declaration of Independence before we ring the dinner bell. After supper, dancing, a bonfire, and a few fireworks."

People gathered in little groups to wander up toward the comfort of the tall trees beside the house. Cal stood beside Maggie as the people around them dispersed. She sagged onto the stands. "I saw it, but I still don't believe it." How must Cal feel about it? Though he'd made light of his relationship with Georgia, he must be at least chagrined to have her openly declare her love for Seb this way.

Cal chuckled and sat beside her, stretching out his boots and crossing his ankles while leaning back on his elbows against the next higher row of seats. "They sure took long enough getting around to admitting they had feelings for each other."

"But they don't like each other a bit." Maggie shook her head. "They're always fighting, and Georgia isn't a bit nice to him when he comes into the café."

His hand closed over hers and squeezed. "Sometimes all that arguing is just to cover up deeper feelings—feelings some might not feel safe letting on that they have." His penetrating gaze set all her nerves jangling. "At least I hope that's what it is."

How could the great outdoors suddenly not have any air at all? His gentle grip on her hand seared her skin. She tried to swallow, to quell the panic beating against the back of her breastbone. She couldn't be falling for him. She wouldn't fall for him. It would be too complicated for words. He was part of her investigation, and she was a law officer. He was handsome, and charming, and altogether too dangerous. *Remember what happened with Michael?*

"But what about you and Georgia? I thought she was in love with you." She loaded her voice with accusation. There. That should put things back onto a safer footing.

He grinned, unrepentant. "That was all an act. Georgia's been in love with Seb for years, and he wasn't exactly coming up to scratch, so she decided to show him he wasn't the only rock on the riverbank. She asked me to play up to her when Seb was around."

"And you went along with it?" Maggie frowned.

"Sure. I don't mind giving romance a little nudge now and again, though I never imagined it would take over a year and a near miss with a bucking horse to make those two declare themselves. I wanted to tell you a couple of times, but I have to admit, you sure were cute when you bawled me out for toying with Georgia's affections."

The warmth in his eyes would melt block ice. She braced herself against it and disengaged her hand from his clasp. "I think I'd better go help Clara and Lily with the dinner preparations." She bolted toward the safety of the house.

When she arrived at Lily's elbow, she tried to take deep breaths, hoping no one would notice how her pulse leaped and her hand trembled when she accepted a cool glass of cider. Cal and Georgia—it was all a ruse. So where did that leave her?

"Maggie. . ." Clara drew her attention. Lily and Alec stood on the porch with her and a stranger. "I'd like you to meet my father, Colonel Bainbridge. This is Maggie Davis. She's staying with Lily right now."

A stately, white-haired man with an upright bearing and forthright handshake smiled beside Clara. "Welcome to the Cross B Ranch." He reached out and chucked Rose under the chin where she perched on Lily's hip. "This little charmer must be the one who found my lower bookshelves after her nap today."

Lily tried to apologize, but Clara laughed. "You'll have to get used to it. We're going to have to move things up higher soon." She laid her hand on top of her mounded waist. "I imagine this baby will be just as inquisitive as Rose."

What would it be like to have a baby growing inside her? To be anticipating with joy the arrival of a child? To have someone—Cal?—look at her with possessive, tender fire in his eyes, a look that shared a private world of two found only in marriage?

A loud *bang* startled her. Several more followed. Cal stood under the overhang of the blacksmith shed near the barn, surrounded by little boys.

"Cal's hitting gunpowder with a hammer on the anvil." Alec shrugged and shook his head. "Look at all those kids." He gave his wife a quick squeeze, shoved his hands into his pockets, and strolled that way.

Clara shaded her eyes and followed him with her gaze. "Grown men are at least half little boy half the time. He can't wait to go try it himself."

Maggie used the diversion to pull herself together and get her thoughts off marriage and babies and Cal. That life wasn't for her.

During the speeches and the reading of the Declaration, she mingled with the crowd, listening for anything that might help her investigation and putting names and faces together. Though the smell of the beef turning on the spit in the yard tantalized her, she found she could only pick at her dinner, highly aware of Cal's location no matter where he moved. Her senses seemed to be charged, her skin sensitive, her hearing acute.

Sheriff Powers wandered through the crowd, much as Maggie did herself, but as she watched him, she realized he had a purpose to his path. He spoke with only the most influential: the ranch owners, the shopkeepers, the businessmen. The cowboys, laborers, and miners, he ignored.

She gave up her surveillance and went to help with the mountain of dishes once more. A dozen women chattered and bustled in and out of the ranch house kitchen. By the time the sound of the musicians tuning up their instruments filtered through the screen door, Maggie was exhausted. She'd argued with herself, scolded herself, and finally given herself an ultimatum. She must stay away from Cal McConnell. She had an investigation to run, and she couldn't trust him. *You don't want to go through that again. This time you might not survive.*

Pleased that she was able to take such a firm grip on herself, she put the last dish back into the cupboard, wiped her hands on the dish towel by the back door, and walked out into the cooling evening air with a plan. She'd steer clear of Cal, keep her mind on work, and when the time came, she would leave Money Creek with her heart and her pride intact.

She strolled toward the music. Paper lanterns waved in the slight evening breeze, bright spots of color strung on lines suspended from poles at each corner of the dance floor. People clustered around the edges of the platform.

Alec strode to the center. "Good evening, folks. I hope you got enough to eat." Several groans and patted stomachs assured him they had. "The winners of each event get first choice of a partner for this evening's dance. So, you cowboys who won today, go pick out your girls for the first dance." He waved to the fiddler, who sawed away at "The Irish Washerwoman."

Maggie clapped to the lively tune, laughing when the cowboy who had won the horse race jogged across the stage and bowed low to a pretty blond girl who blushed and took his hand. Another couple joined them, one of them the stocky fellow who had leaped off his horse onto the back of a running steer in an event Maggie had considered ridiculous, wrestling it to the ground by twisting its snout around over its shoulder until it flopped on its side. The two men who had won the team roping made short work of choosing their partners.

Then Cal stood before her. "May I have the honor?"

She stopped clapping. "You?"

He nodded, the dimple creasing his cheek. "Seb and I were declared the co-winners of the wild horse breaking. He's decided to sit this one out with Georgia. What do you say?"

It's not fair, Lord. You know what I have to do. Why do You make it so hard?

"Maggie?" He held out his hand.

A girl could sink deep into those blue eyes and never surface. Her hand went out to his, and she shivered when their fingers touched.

He tugged, and she followed him up onto the platform. Though others moved around them, they were only vague images on the edge of her vision. Cal's face drew her complete attention, and he fitted her into his arms with ease.

His strong hand spread-eagled on her back, guiding her, and her fingers rested lightly on his broad shoulder. He winked at her and tilted his head as if summing her up and liking what he saw.

She couldn't look away. The power he had over her frightened her into stiffening.

"Relax." He leaned in and whispered against her temple, his breath tangling in her hair. "I'm not going to bite you."

You could do far worse than that, Cal McConnell. You could break my heart.

nine

Maggie hurried out after dark to the meeting place under the trees behind the livery. She was late and hoped Maxwell hadn't gotten too impatient. Lily had asked for Maggie's help rolling out pie crusts for Georgia's order in the morning, and they'd still been in the kitchen well past the time when Maggie should've been meeting the marshal.

Maxwell stood beside the tree, and he wasn't alone. "I was beginning to wonder if you got my letter. Guess the holiday threw things off." Maxwell straightened and uncrossed his arms.

She stayed back, half concealed by the branches. "I picked it up yesterday when I got back to town. I was at the Cross B for the rodeo and picnic the day before."

"Well, come here. You've met Sheriff Powers?"

Maggie wasn't sure who was more surprised.

The sheriff hooked his thumbs through his suspenders and scowled. "*This* is your agent? She's a...a..."

"I think 'woman' is the word you're looking for, Sheriff." Maggie frowned at Maxwell.

"Now, Maggie, before you bite my head off, listen." Maxwell put up his hands as if to ward her off. "You're all alone down here, and I don't like it. The trial's dragging on up in Boise, and I can't get anyone else down here to help you right now. There's been a development you need to know about." He took off his gloves and paired them up before sticking them in the gap between his hip and his gun butt. "But first, what news do you have?"

Maggie blew out a breath. "I'm sure the sheriff has told you already. The stage was robbed again south of here, and three men were killed. Robbers burned the coach and raided the box. Five of the horses were recovered, and the driver will be laid up for at least another month. The sheriff took a posse down." She shrugged. "I couldn't come up with a reason to tag along, so I had to hang out at the café and listen to the talk afterwards. Hecker keeps his mouth shut, which might just be good banking practice or it might mean he's hiding something. Joe Williams is harmless, and frankly, I don't know that he's bright enough to mastermind a gang of thieves unless he's a good actor."

Powers snorted. "Joe Williams is as dumb as a sack of hammers."

Maggie ignored him. "I've gone over the map, and every single stage that has been robbed was either heading into or out of Money Creek and got hit within a forty mile radius. Whoever the gang boss is, he's in this town or nearby. There aren't that many men in the area who could hide that kind of money. Hecker could for sure. Or Colonel Bainbridge possibly. He's got quite a spread out there at the Cross B, and he's heavily invested in several of the mines and in the stage line. I've asked around a little, but no one is spreading an unusual amount of cash."

"Your cover's still good? Did you check out the mercantile?"

"You were right. Mrs. Purdy opened up like a geyser. If anyone had money, she'd know about it. By the way, she's placed three orders with me so far. It's a good thing your sister is a wholesaler and can get us pretty much whatever's ordered. I've had women stopping by Lily's wanting to place orders, too. I've been steering them through Mrs. Purdy's. Keeping on her good side might prove useful. I wouldn't want her to think I was stealing her customers and cutting her out. Between the merchants here and in Silver City, this business is exploding."

Maxwell grinned. "That will make my sister happy. I told you it was a good cover."

"It's terrific. What are you going to tell people when I leave town for good?" Maggie twisted her mouth. "Enough about that. What development do I need to know about?"

Maxwell rubbed his hands together. "Now this isn't exactly rock solid yet, but we might've finally caught a break in the case. You know the two suspects we hauled up to trial? One of them, Stephen Kruger, has been talking a lot. Says he knows something about the stage robberies. He's looking to make a deal."

"What kind of deal? And how solid is not exactly rock solid?" Maggie chewed on the corner of her lip. If ever a case needed a break, it was this one. She was tired of banging her head against walls at every turn.

"I told him I didn't trust him and that he'd better come forth with something I could confirm, or there was no deal."

Powers sucked his teeth. "I sure wish you'd brought me in on this sooner. I might've been able to help. A lot of these robberies have happened on my patch, and I feel like I've been working in the dark. I thought U.S. marshals were supposed to take care of prisoners and hunt down fugitives, not take over local investigations."

"The governor himself called us in. He knows you're spread pretty thin down here, and he's worried that the continuing crime spree will delay any chance Idaho Territory has of becoming a state. He wants this thieving to stop, and he doesn't care who brings the robbers down as long as it gets done."

Maggie tried to put herself in Powers's boots. Truth be told, she knew how he felt. The governor had given him a vote of no confidence by bringing in the marshals, and it sure felt as if Maxwell was doing the same to her by bringing Powers in. She swallowed her hurt feelings and tried to focus. "Where do we go from here?" She directed the question at Maxwell.

"For now, continue as you are. We'll keep working on Kruger on our end. The minute he cracks, we'll jump. Keep digging, and follow whatever leads you can find here."

Powers snorted. "She's following Cal McConnell pretty close. Is that what you had in mind?" He spat out the name McConnell as if he'd bitten into something nasty.

Maxwell went still. "That so, Maggie? Think you're on to something there?"

Grateful for the darkness, Maggie clenched her fists and modulated her voice. "I've found no indication that Cal McConnell is involved in the robberies. It's natural that I would spend time in his company. I ride on his stage twice a week, and I'm staying in his brother's house."

Maxwell ripped a few needles off the pine branch beside his head. "Just be careful there. We've both been fooled before into trusting the wrong man."

Powers cracked his knuckles. "I don't like it. If another stage gets robbed while you're sitting on your hindquarters up there in a courtroom, I'm the one who will get blamed. You won't be the one who has to explain to the mine owners or to the bank how you let their money slip through your fingers. That will be me." He poked his thumb into his chest. "I'm beginning to think the only reason you brought me in on this is because you wanted a scapegoat if you can't catch the robbers."

"Enough." Maxwell stiffened and stood tall, his feet braced apart. "Powers, your job is to watch Maggie's back. Maggie, if you need help with anything before I get back, you go to the sheriff here. I'll be heading out at first light, and between me and Trace, we'll get what we need to know out of Kruger. Until then, keep alert and get word to me if anything changes."

On her way back to Lily's house, Maggie pondered something Maxwell had said. *"We've both been fooled before into trusting the wrong man."*

How foolish was her fledgling trust in Cal McConnell? She stopped at the gate and closed her eyes, wrapping her fingers around the pickets and raising her face to the starlit sky. "Lord, I want to trust him, but I'm afraid. Show me which way to go."

&

Maggie sat on a blanket under a tree behind Lily's house watching Rose toddle around, picking flowers and prattling a steady stream of happy noises. Every few minutes the little girl came to Maggie with a new treasure—a dandelion, a leaf, and this last time, a smooth rock that she handled like a soap bubble. Her eyes grew round, and her mouth formed a perfect O. She placed the pebble in Maggie's palm and said something incomprehensible, then beamed and turned to explore again.

"Well, if it isn't the two prettiest ladies in the world, right here together."

Maggie squeezed the rock and looked up into Cal's eyes. He vaulted the low backyard fence.

Rose spied him and let out a shriek. Her hem tangled around her legs, and she went over in a heap in the longer grass bordering a clump of daisies. The sweet expression vanished into a bellow.

Cal covered the yard in quick strides and scooped her up into the safety and comfort of his arms.

"Now, now, there's no need for all that caterwauling. You just took a tumble." He patted her back, and she burrowed under his chin. He brought her over to Maggie, who had risen as far as her knees then sank back against the tree trunk. Cal eased down and crossed his legs, putting Rose into his lap and pushing his hat back. "I was hoping I'd find you here. Where's Lily?"

"I told her she was working too hard, to go take a nap, and I would watch Rose."

"She's not ailing, is she?" Concern colored his words.

"She's just overtired. Georgia has put in some sizable orders lately, and there's a wedding coming up that she's making the cake for. Rose is really getting around these days. She takes a lot of watching." As if to punctuate this statement, the little girl scrambled off Cal's lap and rushed after a butterfly. "At least back here she's penned in by the fence. I had a hard time getting Lily to let me watch her at all, and I had to promise I wouldn't let her out of my sight." Maggie drew her legs up and wrapped her arms around her knees. She pressed her ankles together, feeling the lump of her gun against the inside of her left calf.

"Makes sense. Lily's still a bit fearful, ever since Rose got kidnapped. She doesn't trust too many folks with Rose, but she trusts you." He smiled, and Maggie had to remind herself not to sigh.

The back door opened, and Lily came out. "I heard Rose cry. Is she all right?"

"So much for getting you to rest." Maggie dropped the warm stone she held into her lap.

Cal nodded. "She's fine. Why don't you go put your feet up? Maggie says you've been working too hard."

"Nonsense. I had a nice little nap. I'll take her inside with me and let you two talk." Lily reached out for the toddler, who grabbed her fingers and walked on tiptoe all the way to the back porch and inside.

"She sure loves that little girl."

"Not that long ago, we all thought we'd never see Rose again." Cal plucked a piece of grass and tore little pieces off it while he talked. "It was God's blessing we got her back unharmed." He tossed the last piece away. "I didn't come here to talk about that though."

The direct look in his blue eyes made Maggie's breath stumble. "You didn't?"

"Nope. I came to talk about us."

Her breath didn't stumble this time. It fell flat and refused to get up. Her heart, in contrast, squeezed hard then raced around her chest. "Us?" She strangled on the word and it came out weaker than she wanted.

"Maggie, I have some powerful feelings for you, and I think you have some for me, too." He reached out and took her hand, searing her palm by brushing his thumb across her skin. "I can sense that you're holding something back from me, that you're afraid. I can understand that. We haven't known each other long, but I want to know everything about you. I've never felt like this about anyone before. I watched my brothers fall in love and get married, and I see how happy they are, how much they love their wives. I promised myself that unless or until I found someone to love like that, I wouldn't ever get married."

Her hand spasmed within his, and she jerked.

"I know, it's a little soon to be talking about marriage, but I want to be honest with you. I love you, Maggie Davis, and I want to marry you, when you're ready, when you think you know me well enough, and when you're ready to trust me. I think I fell in love with you the minute I dumped all that girly stuff out of your suitcase. The way you glared up at me, and later you bawled me out for messing with Georgia's affections. When I held you on the dance floor, well, I just knew I'd never be the same again." He grinned, and a lightheaded vapor swirled through her head. "I look at you, and I start thinking forever kind of thoughts."

She didn't know what to say. Part of her wanted to throw herself into his arms and accept the love he offered her. Part of her wanted to run. Far. And fast. Then he reached out and caressed her cheek. Her heart tumbled. He deserved to know the truth. At least as much of the truth as she could tell him. Because in a blinding flash, she admitted what she had been refusing to acknowledge. She loved him. She was in love with Cal McConnell.

On the heels of this admission came soul-wracking fear. *Lord, is this wise? Can I risk handing my heart over to someone again?* She'd prayed the prayer a hundred times since the Fourth of July, and each time she felt His nudging her to trust, not only Cal but Him. A verse she'd been holding on to came to her mind. *"In God have I put my trust: I will not be afraid what man can do unto me."*

She took a deep breath then took the plunge. "Cal, before you say anything more, there's something you should know about me. I *have* been keeping something back from you." Her throat felt as if someone had stuffed a ball of yarn halfway down it.

"You know you can tell me anything."

If only she could. But she could tell him something.

"What you sensed was right. I have been wary of you, for a lot of reasons. The most important one is because I've been hurt in the past. The man I thought I loved let me down rather badly. Last year was a pretty rough one for me."

Cal laced his fingers with hers and waited, which gave her the courage to say more.

"I was engaged. We were to be married, but he cleared out two weeks before the wedding." She closed her eyes against the wave of pain those memories always caused, but when the hurt came, it was smaller and less acute than ever before. "He stole everything I had, cleaned out my bank account, and left me with a sizable debt. In my ignorance, I let him talk me into changing the names on my bank account and the deed to the house my father left me. I thought it wouldn't matter, since we were going to be married. It seemed like a good thing to do, take care of the details early so I wouldn't be bothered with them when we got back from our wedding trip." Shame burned through her middle. Cal must think her an imbecile.

She swallowed and told the rest. "I learned that I wasn't the first woman he'd swindled this way. Ma—" She faltered on her boss's name. "A friend tracked Michael down and arrested him. Unfortunately, by the time the law caught up with him, he'd squandered everything he stole from me, so there was nothing left to recover. He was already engaged to another woman. She refused to believe the charges against him, and as far as I know, she'll be waiting for him when he gets out of jail in ten years. I got ill soon after that and spent all of last winter and this spring recovering in a cheap boardinghouse on the Montana border."

She dared a glance at him, expecting to see pity. Instead, the muscles in his jaw worked, and his eyelids narrowed until only a sliver of his icy blue eyes showed.

"I'd like to catch up with that fellow. I'd have a few things I'd like to say to him."

She shook her head and tugged a little on his hand. "There's no need for that. He's in jail and will be for a long time. Anyway, that's why I was so prickly when I first met you. I figured a man as handsome and as charming as you had to have some ulterior motive in paying attention to someone like me."

"I'm not going to forget you think I'm handsome, but what

do you mean someone like you?" He tilted his head, and the creases beside his mouth deepened. "You're prettier than the sunshine in the morning. I could never get enough of looking at you, and I sure can't seem to quit thinking about you. This fellow you were engaged to was an idiot, and he deserved to lose you. If you were mine, I'd never let you go." He reached out and caressed her cheek. "That's something you should know about me. I'm mighty possessive."

She blinked and moistened her lips. Her first tentative steps toward trust had her heart near to bursting.

"I don't blame you for being skittish around men, not after what you've been through, but"—he raised her hand and brushed a kiss across the backs of her fingers, holding her gaze the whole time—"I'm not him, and I wouldn't ever treat you that way. I don't give my love easy, but when I do, it's for keeps. You can trust me, Maggie."

Warmth of his lips sank into her skin and melted away the ice around her heart. If a kiss on the hand affected her like this, what would it be like to have him kiss her lips? She had to derail that train of thought before she threw herself into his arms. Unable to speak, she waited, staring into his eyes.

"All this must seem mighty sudden to you, but the truth is I haven't been able to think about much else since I first laid eyes on you. My brothers always told me that if I ever fell for a woman, I'd fall hard and fast. They sure were right." His dimple flashed. "You just got over a heartache, and up until recently, you thought I was stringing Georgia along." He fitted his palm against hers, comparing their hands. "Now that we have everything sorted out, things'll run smooth."

Her conscience smote her. How she wished she was free to tell him the rest, about her job, about her investigative work.

"Cal, there are other things I have to tell you, but I can't right now. I want to, but they involve other people."

An unusual solemnity came over him, giving him a wiser, older look. "Trust is built up slow, I guess. As much as I'd love to know everything about you right this minute, I'd say we've made a good start, and that will do for now."

He scooted closer and took her face in his wide, rough palms. Slowly, giving her plenty of time to pull away if she wanted to, he lowered his lips to hers. Her pulse thundered in her ears as she let him capture her with his kiss.

ten

Cal whistled "The Irish Washerwoman" as he loaded mailbags into the stage boot. Maggie Davis. Who would've thought such a tender woman lived behind those prickles? How glad he was that he'd kept trying to break down those walls. She'd been hurt. No one could blame her for not trusting again. He threw the next mailbag with some force. How he'd like to catch up to the fellow who broke her heart. He would be sorry he'd messed with Cal McConnell's girl.

Cal McConnell's girl. The words sent a shotgun blast of warmth through him, and he couldn't stop grinning. If he walked over to the trough and looked at his reflection, he figured he'd see the same silly grin Alec and Trace wore when they talked about their wives. Whenever he thought about Maggie, his insides turned to mush. Maybe he was rushing his fences a bit, but then again, maybe not.

"You're mighty chipper for this early in the morning, Cal." Joe Williams strolled out onto the boardwalk and stretched. His yawn gave Cal a nice view of his molars.

"Sure enough. You're looking at a happy man." The last bag just fit into the compartment.

"It ain't natural to be that happy this time of day." The ticket agent rubbed his eyes with the heels of his hands.

Cal clapped him on the shoulder. "Maybe you should go to bed earlier."

His grin widened. Maggie appeared at the end of the street with her valise and sales case. If things went the way Cal hoped, she'd be able to give up that job in the not too distant future.

He crossed the distance between them and had to restrain himself from lifting her up in his arms and swinging her around. "I'd kiss you right now if we weren't standing in the middle of the street." He took her bags and fell into step beside her. "You're looking pretty this morning."

The blush that lit her cheeks sent a thrill through him. "I don't know why I was so nervous to see you again this morning. I guess. . ." She brushed a stray hair up from her neck into the bunch at the back of her head. "I guess I thought maybe after you went home yesterday you'd have second thoughts."

He stopped beside the stage and set her bags at his feet. "Maggie, I'm not as fickle as that. When I say something, I mean it." He took her chin in his hand and forced her to look up at him. She was so tiny, so fragile, and knowing the heartache she'd suffered made him want to gather her up and vow to protect her forever, but he wouldn't press her. She needed time to trust him, time for him to show her that his feelings weren't here today and gone tomorrow.

"Time to go!" Joe hollered.

Cal released Maggie and wrenched the door open so she could board. He tossed her bags up to the messenger to stow and made one final check of the team and stage. Duty called. At least with her job right now, she came along on every trip he made to Silver City. He wouldn't have thought just two towns would be a big enough area for a salesperson to cover and make a living, but Georgia had told him almost every woman in town had ordered something through Purdy's. He'd helped Maggie deliver the parcels from the freight office to the mercantile himself. He shrugged when he picked up the lines on the box. What he didn't know about selling women's dainties would fill several books.

The team swung out at a brisk trot in the rapidly warming morning air. "Another scorcher, huh?" He turned to the messenger. "Don't believe we've had the pleasure. Name's Cal."

"Adams." The grunt and the glare declared Adams a man of few words.

Cal shrugged. As long as the man could do his job. He shook up the lines and cajoled the team.

Nearly halfway to Silver City, a few miles past the relay station, the river took a hard turn to the north, and the road along with it. The roadside fell away sharply down to the water's edge on the left, and on the right, an arrowhead of rock jutted out from a hill, forcing a double-back turn before beginning the long trek into Silver City.

Cal climbed the reins, slowing the team as the bend came into sight. "This is usually where the passengers wonder if I'm going to scrape some paint off the side of the coach." Cal flicked a glance at his silent companion.

Adams had his shotgun against his chest and his arms crossed around it. His red beard covered his neck and collar, and his eyelids were slits.

Cal nudged him. "Sunshine sure can make a man sleepy." He'd have to tell Joe that Adams might not be the best express guard in the world, what with his snoozing the whole trip. The only time the man had roused was to climb down and have a cup of coffee at the relay station while they changed horses.

Cal guided the team closer to the rock wall and slowed their trot until they were almost walking.

The off leader threw up his head and balked as they neared the turn. "Easy there, Wally." The dark bay sidled and snorted, jostling his trace partner and unsettling the entire team. Reluctantly, crab-stepping and snorting, the horses rounded the corner. Cal pulled back on the lines and leaned on the brake pedal. Dread hit his gut and coursed through him.

A pile of rocks almost as high as the lead horses' noses barred the way. Atop the pile, a masked man sat holding a rifle aimed at Cal. Behind him, two more masked riders sat on their horses, guns trained on the coach. They held the reins to another horse that caught Cal's attention—a shaggy pinto. The man on the rock pile narrowed his eyes.

Lord, what do we do now? Please, protect us and protect Maggie. Cal's throat, already dry, parched further. Maggie.

"Afternoon." The outlaw glanced up at the sun. A slight breeze fluttered the faded red bandana across the lower half of his face. "Took you long enough to get here."

"Sorry to inconvenience you, Hack. I know how you hate to be kept waiting." Cal's hands tightened on the reins. A quake started in his middle. The last few holdups, the violence had gotten worse. Passengers murdered, coach burned.

Adams, now wide awake, swallowed hard enough for Cal to hear. "You fellows are blocking our path."

Hack cackled. "Well now, you're right about that." He motioned to the outlaws flanking him. "You got something we want. I believe we'll be getting it now." The two men dismounted and picked their way over the pile. They had to sidle past the stage horses, one on either side of the team.

Cal's hand fingered the butt of his gun. He glanced at Adams, whose skin stood out pasty white against the dark red of his beard. His hands shook on the shotgun. No help there. The man was a quivering mess. He'd be useless in a fight, and there was no way, with the road blocked, that Cal could whip up the team to try to outrun them. Not even any way to turn the coach around on this narrow road. A perfect little ambush.

Hack stood and pointed his rifle at Cal's chest. "Everybody out of the coach, and you boys climb down from there, too. Leave the guns."

Adams dropped his gun like he'd been scalded and all but fell off the box. Cal took his time, wrapping the reins, stalling, trying to think of a way out of this, and all the while his anger mounted. He stood on the box and slowly drew his revolver.

"Easy now. Just lay it on the seat like a good boy."

Cal seethed climbing down, but he had to keep his head. The minute his boots hit the rocky road, one of the gunmen shoved him in the shoulder. "Get back there with the others."

He rounded the coach. Maggie and the two male passengers stood in a row along the rock wall. The men had their hands up at about shoulder level, eyes wide. Easterners in nice new suits and not a gun between them. Cal hadn't thought much about either one when they'd boarded the stage this morning. Just a couple of strangers passing through. They'd been polite to Maggie and quiet at the midday stop.

A burst of fear bloomed in Cal's chest at Maggie's defiant stance. Her heart-shaped face exuded confident anger, and her eyes snapped fire. He didn't want her drawing attention to herself, perhaps giving Hack a reason to single her out. He edged close to her. "Easy, Maggie. Let them do what they came to do, and hopefully they'll take off."

She unclenched her fists and crossed her arms at her waist. "We need to stop them." Her low voice pricked across his skin.

He didn't see how he could do anything about it without getting someone killed. His passengers—and Maggie in particular—had to be his first priority. If they kept their heads, Hack would just take the contents of the express box and run. Cal knew all too well Hack's willingness to harm a woman, and he couldn't allow anything like that to happen to Maggie. "No, we need to let them do what they came to do and let them go."

Hack stood atop the stage and aimed his shotgun at the express box. "Hold that lead team, will you?" he called down to one of his men. "And you, keep your gun trained on those passengers." He pointed to the other at the rear of the stage.

"I don't want anything stupid to happen like last time just because you got careless."

Hack's shot reverberated off the rocks, and the coach lurched when the horses tried to bolt. Hack got knocked onto the seat but quickly regained his feet. The hinges on the box creaked, and he crowed, looking down. "It's here. Just like he said it would be. Lookit this." He held up a silver bar that shot back the sun's rays in a white flash. With a flip, he turned the bar over to study the mark on the end. "More than ten thousand dollars in silver from the Henderson Mine, and"—he bent again—"bank notes." A breeze fluttered the ends of the bills he held up for his compatriots to see. He scanned the top of the coach and picked through the baggage. "This will do."

Maggie gasped as Hack grabbed her suitcase and opened it. When he tipped it up, the contents, all that carefully folded lingerie, tumbled out and fell from the top of the coach into a heap on the dusty road.

Her gasp drew Hack's attention.

Cal's hands tightened into fists, and he edged in front of Maggie, forcing her behind him with his hand on her side.

"Mmmphh."

Cal turned to his right at the sound.

Adams leaned against the rock wall, pressing his palm to his chest. His skin had taken on a gray pallor, and globs of sweat rolled down his temples and darkened his beard.

"What's the matter?" Cal nudged him.

"Heart." Adams forced the words out through gritted teeth. He started to sag, his knees buckling, and Cal reached out to brace his broad shoulders against the rock. "Bad heart."

"Help me." Cal jerked his head to one of the male passengers who stood frozen, his hands still shoulder-high. The gunman covering them lowered his rifle a fraction.

"Hey," the robber called up to Hack who was stuffing

money and silver into Maggie's emptied suitcase. "We got some trouble back here."

"Well, handle it. I'm busy. And while you're at it, get their valuables. No point in leaving anything behind."

Adams's weight sagged as Cal struggled to brace him and lower him to the ground without injury. The man had gone limp and couldn't help at all.

Maggie, ignoring the gunman's order to stay still, grasped the unconscious man's head to keep it from jouncing off the rocks on the way to the ground.

"Gotta loosen his collar." Cal placed his hand over Adams's heart.

"Hey, you two, stand back up here. What's wrong with him?" The outlaw's voice sounded high and uncertain, like a scared youngster.

"Do be quiet. Can't you see this man is sick?" Maggie glared at him then returned her attention to Adams.

Cal had to admire her grit, but he wished she wouldn't antagonize them. He unbuttoned the man's collar. Adams's breath rattled in his throat, and his massive chest rose and fell, but then his breathing staggered and all movement stopped.

Maggie lowered her head and pressed her ear to his chest. Her eyes closed and her eyebrows pinched in concentration. After a moment she sat back on her heels. Her eyes sought out Cal's, and she gave her head a little shake.

A pair of boots appeared at the edge of Cal's vision. "What are you doing back here?" Hack set the suitcase down and shoved his fellow thief with the butt of his rifle. "What's wrong with him? I didn't hear any shooting. Did you knife him?"

"No, he just grabbed his chest and keeled over." The young outlaw shook his head so hard his kerchief started to slip. He shoved it back to the bridge of his nose.

Hack's head swiveled toward Cal and Maggie, and he

casually aimed his rifle from the waist. It just happened to line up with Maggie.

Cal rose from beside Adams and interposed himself between the gun and the girl. This was his fault. If he'd caught up to Hack the last time he'd been chasing him, none of this would've happened. Now Maggie was in danger because of it.

An interested spark lit Hack's eyes. "Hmm. What have we here, Cal? You stay right where you are." He stepped sideways until he could see Maggie once more. He shoved the two men passengers out of his way. They skittered back like scared mice. "You two start walking back to Money Creek, and don't turn around or I'll bore you." He motioned toward the road behind them. With a hasty glance at each other, they took off, abandoning Cal and Maggie without even an apologetic look.

"That leaves just us, Cal." Hack's grip on his rifle tightened. "Us and the girl." He nudged the suitcase with the toe of his boot and spoke to the man who had been covering the passengers. "You, get this on my horse and wait up front till I get there." While the bandit loaded the plunder, Hack shoved down his bandana to expose a leer. "No need to stand on ceremony now, is there, Cal? Not old friends like us."

Maggie sucked in a sharp breath behind him.

Cal seethed at being face to face with Hack after all this time. This man who had hurt Clara and Lily, had helped in the kidnapping of Rose, had murdered an unarmed woman and badly beaten another, and had been involved in at least two stage robberies now. Robberies that included the murders of three men and the severe injuring of another, and he had Maggie in his sights. "You got what you came for, Hack. You should get out of here before someone comes along."

"You do have a point. I am in a bit of a hurry today. A shame that, for I'd love to linger with the lady. I just wanted to say thank you for making this holdup the easiest one I've had yet. It helps to be working with someone you know." He grinned and spit. "See you soon, Cal."

⋅❧⋅

A shroud of disbelief wrapped Maggie in its folds. They knew each other? They called each other by name. Hack. He had lowered his bandana, not even caring that Maggie saw his face.

When the sound of hoofbeats faded, Cal smacked his fist into his palm. He looked at Maggie. "Are you all right?"

"Yes." *Except for what I'm thinking now. Except for the fact that the robber called you by name. Except for the fact that you knew his name.*

Had her instincts been off again? The hollow feeling in her chest expanded a notch. She took a grip on her stampeding thoughts. No, there was an explanation for this. She would give him a chance to explain before jumping to conclusions. The Cal she knew wasn't a stage robber.

What could she have done differently? Drawn her gun? The two-shot derringer wouldn't have done her much good. Anything less than a Gatling gun wouldn't have done much good, not with three-to-one odds.

Cal took off his hat and swiped his forearm across his brow. "I'd best get busy moving rocks."

"I'll help you."

"You'd be better off waiting in the shade."

"Waiting in the shade won't get us moving again." She followed him along the side of the coach, hanging on to the wheel, the door handle, edging by and not looking down the steep drop-off to the water below.

Jagged boulders, most the size of loaves of bread, lay in a tumbled heap. A fresh scar of lighter rock showed on the wall above them.

"They must've dynamited off a chunk then piled up the

scattered bits." Maggie's investigative mind forced its way through the fog in her head. "Bold."

"Hack's a bold fellow." Cal picked up a rock and chucked it over the hill before reaching for another.

"How is it you know him?" The words came out casually, as if his answer didn't hold her happiness in the balance.

The next boulder went cascading down toward the river with more force. "I've had a couple run-ins with him before. Last fall he was part of the crew that kidnapped Rose. I almost had him, was chasing him down in fact, when a bolt of lightning struck. It felled a tree right in front me. I went east and my horse went west. I felt like a complete greenhorn. If it wasn't for getting thrown, I'd have caught Hack."

"He knew your name." She hated the accusation in her voice but couldn't stop it. "He didn't care if you saw his face."

He froze then slowly straightened. His eyes hardened into icy blue chips. "Margaret Davis, I want you to listen to me." His hands settled on his lean hips. "Hack wanted me to see his face because he wanted to rub it in that I haven't been able to stop him from doing pretty much whatever he wanted in this territory. He's robbed, rustled, kidnapped, murdered, and terrorized from here to Boise. And not me, nor Sheriff Powers, nor the U.S. marshals themselves have been able to do a blessed thing about it. As for him knowing me by name"—his hands came up in a frustrated gesture—"I'm a stage driver. Everybody knows my name. It's part of the job. People I've never met call me by name all the time."

Her heartbeat slowed, and guilt pressed on her shoulders. Hack had leered at Cal, almost daring him to do something to stop him. She'd witnessed strangers greeting Cal on the streets of Silver City. She knew the names of several of the drivers on the line herself, though she didn't know the men themselves.

"I'm sorry, Cal. You're right. I shouldn't have doubted you."

She bent to pick up a rock.

His hands closed over her shoulders and he brought her up gently against his chest. "You're just all churned up. I'm sure it looked bad, but"—he put his finger against her chin and lifted her face so she had to look in his eyes—"Maggie, I wouldn't ever mislead you. You can trust me. I'm just glad you weren't hurt. Hack's a killer, and he wouldn't have batted an eye if he'd have shot us both right there on the road."

She allowed the warmth of his embrace, the strength of his arms, and the steady beating of his heart against her palms to comfort and reassure her. This was Cal, the man she loved. She could trust him.

eleven

They reported the robbery in Silver City, and Maggie slipped a letter to Maxwell onto the coach headed for Boise. Seeing to the remains of the express messenger, Adams, wasted another day. Exhausted and with frayed nerves, she returned to Money Creek with Cal late in the afternoon.

Lily greeted them at the gate with good news. Clara and Alec's baby had arrived, a healthy baby boy. The following day, Cal took Lily and Rose to the Cross B for a visit.

Maggie declined Cal's invitation to go with them. "They won't want a stranger in the house right now. It should just be family."

Cal threaded his fingers through hers and bent to whisper in her ear. "You can be family the minute you give the word." His voice rumbled and sent a tickly feeling through her.

Maggie longed to grasp at the happiness he offered, to throw away caution and embrace a future with Cal McConnell, but she couldn't. Not until this case was finished, not until she was free to tell him the truth about herself. "I'll see you when you get back tomorrow. Give my best wishes to Alec and Clara."

With Lily and Rose looking on, Cal didn't kiss her good-bye, but the intent gleam in his eyes told her that was the only reason he restrained himself.

Maggie saw Cal and Lily off and walked up the street for a cup of Georgia's coffee and a chat. She'd just reached the Rusty Bucket when Powers pulled his horse up at the hitching post.

"Morning, Miss Davis. I was hoping I'd run into you."

"Sheriff." Why was he approaching her in broad daylight?

He was about as subtle as a bucket of water in the face. He'd blow her cover for sure.

His saddle creaked when he dismounted, and his horse shifted away from him. Powers reached up into his hatband for a toothpick and stuck it between his teeth. "I figured you'd be in to make your report when you got back to town yesterday."

"Keep your voice down. I can't just sashay up to the jail under the eyes of the town."

He narrowed his eyes. "Then do it after dark. It's about time you started treating me like a partner in this investigation. I want to hear everything you know about this last holdup."

Give me patience, Lord.

After her coffee at the Rusty Bucket, where Georgia was too busy to sit and talk, Maggie spent some time chatting with Joe Williams at the stage office. She also engineered an "accidental" meeting with Hecker from the bank when they both happened to enter Purdy's Mercantile at the same time. Joe and Hecker each expressed their disgust and frustration at the latest robbery, solicitous for her welfare, sorry she'd been on the stage when it got held up. If either of them was in on the thieving, he didn't let on.

With no breaks in the case, she pinned a lot of hope on Maxwell and Trace being able to get information out of Kruger. She went back to Lily's and tried to ignore how impatient and restless she felt and how much she missed Cal. She finally went to the back porch and fell asleep on the swing.

She awakened well after dark, disoriented and stiff. With a groan, she hurried into the house to fix her hair and grab a shawl before heading to the jail.

Powers sat behind his scarred old desk, his boots resting on the corner. He held a stack of wanted posters, perusing each one before adding it to the pile on his lap.

She shut the door and lowered the shawl from her hair.

"You're late. It's almost midnight. Dallying with McConnell?"

"Cal isn't even home. He drove out to the Cross B this morning." His belligerence set her teeth on edge. He wasn't her boss, and she was in charge of this investigation. High time he knew that. "Let's get this over with." She kept her tone crisp and businesslike.

He motioned to the chair at the end of the desk. "Fine. Go ahead."

She took the seat and recited the order of incidents, everything from the rock pile to Adams's collapse.

Powers listened to it all, though his expression bespoke his boredom. As she neared the end of the recitation, he lowered his feet and raised one eyebrow at her. "So, what you're saying is the stage got robbed in spite of you. I thought your job was to stop the robberies. Highwaymen can do whatever they want in this territory if you're the only thing standing in their way."

Maggie clenched her hands in the shawl fringe in her lap. "My job is to gather information, to seek out clues. There was no way I could have stopped that holdup. If I would've tried, innocent people would've been killed."

"You're right. You'd have all been dead, which is why I don't hold with women in this line of work. You're being paid to gather information, but all you do is gum up the investigation tagging along behind Cal McConnell." He scratched his cheek. "You haven't brought me a single thing I can use. Not that I expected you would."

She took a grip on her temper. "You interrupted me before I could tell you the rest. Do you want to hear it or not?"

He shrugged, pricking her anger again. Insufferable male. "Go ahead, but make it quick. I'd like to be in bed. If you hadn't been so late, I'd be asleep right now."

Counting to ten really didn't work very well. With Powers

she'd probably have to count to a thousand, and she'd still feel like kicking him in the backside. "I can identify one of the robbers."

Powers jerked upright. "What? Why didn't you say so? Who is it?" He shifted in his chair and put his hand on his gun.

A shiver trickled down Maggie's spine. "His name is Hack. I'd guess he was about five foot nine, with dark brown hair and brown eyes. He rides a shaggy pinto, black and white. He knew Cal by name, and Cal knew him. Evidently they've had a run-in bef—"

Powers lunged forward in his chair, eyes gleaming. "They knew each other?" He ran his tongue around his teeth and made a sucking sound.

"Yes, last fall when—"

She jumped when he snapped his fingers. "That's it. You've found the link."

"The link?"

"Of course." He snorted and rolled his eyes. "How the robbers are getting tipped off. Cal's one of them. I knew it." He rubbed his hands together. "I always suspected Cal, but I never could find a way to pin it on him. He made a mistake this time." Powers flicked her a glance. "I suppose you were of some use after all."

"Wait a minute. This isn't proof. I told you, Cal had met him before. Last fall when Rose McConnell was kidnapped." Maggie put her hand flat on the desk and leaned forward. With her other hand, she fingered the chain around her neck. "And anyone could know Cal's name. It isn't exactly a secret. If I was a stage robber, I'd make sure I knew everything I could about the driver, the same way I'd learn everything I could about the route, the schedule, and the contents of the express box."

Powers shuffled through the papers on his desk. "I'm going

to need a search warrant. For his room. Have to talk to the judge." He aimed a hard stare at her. "And don't you give me any sass over it. I've seen you dallying with him. And I don't care what you told Maxwell. It's plain as a pumpkin that you've set your cap for him. You've lost whatever objectivity you might've had. Women always snarl things up with this kind of nonsense."

Indignation burned Maggie's throat. "You're not listening to me. Cal isn't involved in the robberies. He explained to me how he knows Hack. You should be focusing your attention on finding the thieves and stop trying to blame someone who is innocent."

Powers slapped the desk and rose to tower over her. "Cal McConnell is as guilty as sin, and I mean to see he goes to jail. If you stand in my way, I'll arrest you."

She stood and glared up at him. "If you're going to have his room searched, I'm going to be there. The only reason I would ever agree to this is because I know a search of his room will turn up nothing and prove Cal's innocence. But everything happens by the book, or you'll be the one explaining before a judge. You don't enter his room without me."

"McConnell's out of town. No time like the present. I'll go roust the judge and let him decide whether to issue a warrant or not."

"It's the middle of the night. Can't it wait until morning?"

"Nope. I want it taken care of now. Judge Merrill lives just over behind the blacksmith's shop. You wait here, and I'll get the warrant."

"I'd rather go with you."

"The judge is an old man, and he doesn't like women. You'll be doing your cause more harm than good by showing up there in the middle of the night. He's an old friend of mine. I take exception to you thinking I can't do my job. You know if you weren't sweet on McConnell, and you'd brought this information in, you would've been the first one to want a warrant."

Stung, Maggie realized he was right, but she knew Cal. He was innocent. Perhaps a warrant was the best way to prove it. They wouldn't find anything in Cal's room, and they could turn their attention to finding this Hack fellow. "Fine, but I go in on the search with you if the judge grants the warrant."

He scowled at her. "That's what I have deputies for."

"Either I help with the search, or I wire Maxwell and apprise him of the state of the investigation. He will probably advise waiting until he can get back here to supervise himself." Relief flooded her. "That's what I advise, too—waiting until Maxwell returns. He might've cracked that witness, Kruger. Then we'll know where to look next."

Powers shook his head. "I'm an officer of the law, and I've been given specific information that ties a member of this community to a crime. I'd be shirking in my duties if I didn't pursue this lead. I can't risk him hiding the evidence. If Maxwell knew how close you've become with a possible suspect, he'd take you off the case and tell me to proceed."

Maggie bit the side of her thumbnail. In that, Powers was right. One thing Maxwell had always praised about Maggie was her ability to be an objective voice in an investigation. If he knew how she felt about Cal, he'd yank her off the case in less time than it took to send the telegram.

Powers headed for the door. "Sit tight. I'll be back with the papers, and we can get some answers."

So Maggie waited. And paced. And waited some more. How long could getting a warrant take? Her loyalty to Cal and her loyalty to Maxwell warred in her middle, making her nauseous. Almost two hours later, Powers returned, and his eyes glowed with triumph.

"What took you so long?"

He scowled. "The judge is an old man. He doesn't rush anything. Anyway, I had to lay everything out for him so he wouldn't think I wasn't playing fair. Then the judge had to think about it for a while. Then he had to write out the paper. These things are wordy, you know."

"Let me see the warrant."

"There's no time for that. He signed it, see?" He flipped open the heavy paper. The judge's spidery scrawl decorated the bottom. "Says we can search Cal's room over the Rusty Bucket." He stuffed the paper into his vest. "If you're coming with me, then hurry up or I'll go myself. I'll stop by the blacksmith's for a pry bar on the way."

She refused to give in to the fear that Cal might be guilty. This search would prove his innocence. She wasn't going to be a prisoner to her doubts. She trusted Cal. She trusted that God had brought them together. She wouldn't fear what Powers or this search warrant could do to them. "You won't need a pry bar. Cal leaves the door unlocked so if his father needs a place to sleep when Cal's out of town he can get in."

A knowing sneer tugged at the corners of his face. "I *knew* you were getting thick with him. Been up to his place a few times, have you?"

Maggie straightened to her full height, still a head shorter than Powers, and glared. "Keep your foul opinions to yourself, Powers. I haven't been to his room."

"I'll get some tools anyway. Never know what we might run into." Powers carried the lantern.

Maggie followed, her footsteps heavy. How was she going to explain this to Cal? Even though she knew they wouldn't find anything in his rooms, she'd have to think of a way to tell Cal about her real job and the ongoing investigation. Though telling him might be easier if she waited until Maxwell and Trace returned. They would back her up, help show Cal how keeping her identity a secret was in everyone's best interest.

They clomped up the back stairs of the Rusty Bucket. Powers didn't wait for her but flung the door open and stalked in, holding a lantern high. "Check the mattress. I'll look in the bureau."

Maggie surveyed the small space Cal called home. Opposite the door, under the peak, a bed sat under the only window. She lit the lamp on the box beside the bed and, with a feeling of sorrow at invading Cal's privacy like this, lifted the pillow and shook it.

Cal's scent, that indefinable aroma that was just Cal, rose from the ticking. Leather, soap, outdoors. A lump formed in her throat. She ran her hands over the quilt, pressing the mattress. The bedsprings squeaked and gave, but she turned up nothing. The crate that served as his nightstand revealed nothing. A couple of handkerchiefs, a few coins, a picture of Cal with his brothers. She turned the image toward the lamp. Alec and Trace were seated, their rifles across their laps, and Cal stood behind, also holding a rifle. They all looked young, Cal not more than eighteen in the picture. There was a wildness about them, something untamed in their eyes. This must've been taken before they went to the Cross B, before God changed their lives. About the time they went to jail.

"Nothing over here. What about you?" Powers's face appeared sinister in the flickering lantern light.

She returned the photograph. "No. Nothing." Just as she'd expected.

"What about the trunk?"

A domed wood and metal trunk sat at the foot of the bed. "I haven't gotten there yet."

"Well, quit dawdling."

She knelt before the trunk. "It's locked."

Powers brought the lantern. "Told you we'd need the pry bar. Stand back."

"Don't. You'll ruin the lock if you do that."

"I don't care. I'm after evidence."

"Well, I *do* care. I can open the lock without breaking it." She reached behind her neck and unclipped her necklace. With a few deft twists, she freed the long links from one another, revealing a set of lock picks.

"You're full of surprises."

She ignored him and selected one of the probes. It was a simple lock, and it clicked open in a matter of seconds. When she raised the lid, Powers lifted the lantern to see inside. The tang of cedar pricked her nose. The interior of the trunk had been lined with the pungent wood to discourage moths.

The meager contents wrung Maggie's heart. A couple extra sets of clothes. A dark suit with white shirt and starched collar carefully wrapped in brown paper. A shiny pair of black boots, the leather butter soft, and a varnished wooden box.

"What's that?" Powers pointed to the oak box. He reached in and picked it up. It must've been heavier than he'd anticipated, because he grunted and readjusted his grip. He balanced it on the lip of the trunk. "Open it."

"It looks like a jewelry box." Though what Cal would want with one mystified her. "It's locked."

"That shouldn't be hard for you. You got the trunk open quick enough." He stepped back when she rose and lifted the box to sit on the bedside.

Once they'd checked this last thing, they could get out of Cal's room, and she'd blister Powers for doubting him and her. Perhaps she should make the trip up to Boise and meet with Maxwell herself. She'd tell him about Hack, and Maxwell would begin the manhunt. She would be finished and able to tell Cal everything.

While her mind spun these ideas, her fingers probed with the smallest of the lock picks, testing the tumblers and feeling her way through the sequence. This lock, though small, was more sophisticated than the one on the trunk and took her a full two minutes to open.

Powers breathed through his mouth, raspy and moist, while she worked.

The lock finally clicked, and she withdrew the picks and opened the lid. Shock caused her heart to trip. Nestled on a soft bed of ruby velvet lay a single silver bar. She wanted to slam the lid, to hide it behind her back and shield it from Powers. She wanted to scream and throw the box against the wall. She wanted to cry.

Powers grabbed the bar, turning it toward his lantern. "Look at that. That stamp belongs to the Henderson Mine Stamp Mill." He turned it so she could see the HM in a circle pressed into the ingot. "This came from the stage you were on three days ago."

She didn't want to believe it, and yet, her mind saw Hack standing triumphantly atop the stage brandishing a Henderson Mine bar of silver. "Are you sure? It couldn't have come from anywhere else?"

"Believe what's right in front of your eyes, girl." Powers let his exasperation and exultation show. He turned the bar in his hand, feeling the heft. "This must've been Cal's payoff, his share of the take." He pointed. "That jewelry box rings a bell, too. I seem to remember it being listed among the items stolen off the Elko stage a while back. Looks like this silver hasn't been his only payoff."

Numbness crept through Maggie. She lowered the lid on the jewelry box. Once again her instincts had been off. She'd been duped by another handsome charmer.

❧

Midafternoon, Cal urged the horses on, eager to get back to town and to Maggie. Not that seeing his brand-new nephew wasn't a good reason to be away from her, but he'd missed her every minute he'd been gone. She would've gone with him if they had already been married—

He pulled himself up short. He had yet to formally propose to her, though he'd made his intentions clear. He'd best put his mind to getting a ring and thinking up some special way to put the question to her.

Cal stopped the wagon in front of Lily's house and hopped down. He reached up for Lily's waist and swung her down before turning back for Rose who stood in the wagon box, her eyes and nose and fingertips showing as she clutched the top board. "C'mere, punkin."

Lily opened the gate. "Rose seems like such a big girl now that we've seen Brett. Though, come to think of it, he isn't so little after all. Almost nine pounds."

"Alec was fit to bust his buttons." Cal tweaked Rose's nose and lifted her over the side, tickling her a bit and enjoying the reaction. "Clara looked spent though. I hope Alec makes her stay in bed for a while. The newest McConnell male is already filling up those little nightgowns you took for him. Won't be long before he's flanking and flopping calves like his daddy." Cal turned and almost ran into Lily who still stood in the gateway, eyes wide and mouth open.

"Cal McConnell, you're under arrest for robbery and murder." Sheriff Powers's voice stabbed the air.

Lily gasped, and Cal froze.

"Give the baby to Miz McConnell, Cal, and come on with us." Jack West's voice came from behind Cal. He cleared his throat. "We don't want no trouble. Especially not with the baby and Miz Lily here."

Cal eased around, his hand bracing Rose's back, cradling her to him.

Powers and his deputy stood near the back of the wagon. Jack aimed his rifle at the ground, stance relaxed, but Powers had his handgun pointed right at Cal's chest.

Anger galloped through Cal like a runaway team. "What's this about, boys?" As he spoke, he handed Rose off to Lily and made a "back up" motion with his hand. Lily stepped up the path.

Powers advanced a couple of steps. "I'll take your gun. You keep your hands up where we can see them." He took Cal's handgun and stuck it into his own belt. He withdrew a piece of paper from his back pocket and waved it in front of Cal. "I got a search warrant for your room last night, and stolen items were found. Come peaceful down to the jail and don't give us any trouble." His stale breath blew across Cal's face, smelling of old coffee and tobacco. Cal winced when Powers wrenched his hands down and clapped on wrist irons. "I had a notion it was you behind these robberies. I bet you thought I wouldn't figure it out."

"There's some mistake here. I haven't stolen anything. What did you find? And how did you get a warrant for my room?"

"Save it for when we get to the jail."

"Cal, what's going on?" Lily hugged Rose tight enough that the little girl squirmed.

"I don't know, but don't worry. It's some kind of mistake."

Powers jerked Cal's arm, wrenching the handcuffs. "Enough palavering. Let's go."

Cal shouted back over his shoulder to Lily who stood frozen by the wagon. "Find Maggie and tell her what happened. Tell her I'll come see her as soon as I get this cleared up."

Powers's laugh made Cal's skin crawl. Jack shot Cal a sympathetic look then positioned his eyes forward.

Heat clawed up Cal's chest and neck and rushed toward his face when he realized Powers was marching him right down Main Street toward the jail. Townsfolk stopped on the sidewalks and stood in doorways gaping.

Georgia barged out of the café. "Albert Powers, what are you doing?"

"I'm taking my prisoner to jail."

"For what?"

"He's wanted for stage robbing." Powers kept walking.

Georgia hustled alongside. "That's ridiculous."

Cal's heart warmed at her championship. He could always count on Georgia to stick up for him. "Georgia, go see Lily. She needs to get word to Alec and the colonel, but I don't want her driving to the ranch herself."

"Seb's here in town. He'll go." Georgia nodded, her orange topknot threatening to burst loose from its pins.

They reached the jailhouse, and Powers tugged Cal up the steps.

Georgia followed every step of the way. "Anything else I can do for you?"

"Just get Alec here, and then go be with Lily and Maggie until we get this straightened out. Go easy telling Maggie. She doesn't know yet."

Again Powers cackled.

Cal ducked and entered the jail.

Maggie sat in the chair beside the desk, her heart-shaped face white as milk. Her shoulders sagged, and her blue eyes pierced him with a look so wounded Cal flinched. Beside her on the desk, a fancy, lined wooden box stood open, and next to it, a silver bar shone in the block of light coming in the window. Maggie lifted her chin and pressed her lips together. Dark circles hovered under her eyes.

"McConnell, you know Miss Davis. Or should I say Agent Davis?" Powers holstered his gun and hoisted his hip onto the corner of the desk.

"Agent?" Cal looked from one to the other. Bewilderment at the rapid change of events kept the word from sinking in.

"Sure, Agent Maggie Davis, United States Marshal's Office." The sheriff laughed again and slapped his knee, smirking. "When Maxwell told me he had sent in a special investigator, I never dreamed it would be a woman." He swiped his face with his hand. "I didn't think she could do the job, but boy, was I ever wrong. Without her, we never would've nabbed you."

Something that had been strong and steady inside Cal crumbled to dust at Powers words. Her hurt, defiant, accusing expression bludgeoned him.

Jack set his rifle in the rack on the wall and gave an easy tug to Cal's elbow. "C'mon. Let's get you in a cell so we can get these cuffs off. I'm going to need you to remove your holster, too."

"Not until I get some answers." Cal shrugged away. "Maggie? What's this about you and Maxwell?"

She moistened her lips and stood but wouldn't look at him. "I'm an agent for the U.S. marshals. I work for Maxwell, who brought me in on this case. Maxwell felt there had to be an inside man feeding information to the robbers. My job was to ride the stage, to be his eyes and ears here in Money Creek and in Silver City, and find the leak." She might have been discussing the weather for all the emotion her voice showed, though her every word stabbed like a dagger.

"And you think it's me?" Incredulity laced his words. "Why? Why would you think that?" He loathed the handcuffs that kept him from grabbing her shoulders and demanding she look at him.

Powers hefted his bulk upright and snatched the silver bar from the desk. "This. We found this in your room, locked in this box." He jabbed his fat finger at the wooden box. "Stamped with Henderson's mark. Fresh off the Money Creek stage. Your slice of the goods." He hitched his belt. "Get him into a cell while I lock this stuff up."

Once again Cal jerked away from Jack's grasp. "I've never seen those things in my life." He implored Maggie with his eyes to believe him, but she kept her face turned toward the window. "You can't think I had anything to do with the holdups. I was in town when the Elko stage was robbed, and

I was on the stage to Silver City, and so were you, when the thieves showed up."

Powers looked up from where he stowed the silver and the box in a deep desk drawer. He removed some papers from his vest and snorted. "You didn't need to be there. You just fed them the information they needed to get the job done. They knew exactly when the pickings would be good. And"—he glared triumphantly—"one of the outlaws knew you. Called you by name. Not only that, but you called him by name as well. That little slip was all it took. I had a warrant within a couple hours of Maggie making her report." He waved the papers and stuffed them in the drawer.

Another icy cold saber sliced into Cal's heart.

Hack.

He'd explained to Maggie how he happened to know the outlaw's name. She had believed him. Or so he had thought. A spy for Maxwell? Had everything about her been a fraud?

This time he allowed Jack to lead him to a cell and remove his gun belt. After his handcuffs came off, he sagged onto the cot and put his head into his hands. *God, help me.*

⁂

Maggie walked out into the sunshine and shivered. She crossed her arms and gripped her elbows. Every word of accusation had caved her chest in a little more until now it felt empty and broken. Even after several hours to sift through the information of Cal's guilt, she still couldn't believe it. Yet, she'd held the evidence in her own hand, had taken it from the locked trunk herself.

She didn't know where to go. Lily surely wouldn't want to receive her into the house. Powers had said he would arrest Cal at Lily's place as soon as he returned from the ranch. Maggie suspected Georgia wouldn't want to see her either, not Cal's champion in all things.

The telegraph office. She needed to send a wire to Maxwell.

Her cover was blown sky-high, so she was free to communicate by wire with her boss. Maxwell would deal with things from here, just as he always did.

Maggie would have to look for a new line of work. Clearly she had lost whatever edge she had once possessed. Her intuition, her instincts, they were all off. First Michael had duped her; then she'd gotten herself shot; then Cal had walked right into her life and stolen her heart, only to turn out to be a complete maverick. If she continued on as an investigator, it was only a matter of time until she got herself or some innocent bystander killed.

twelve

Cal sagged on the bunk.

Jack handed a cup of coffee to him through the bars. "Hey, you look like you could use this."

The brown liquid tasted like Jack had thrown in a couple of shotgun shells to settle the grounds, but it was warm, and though the sun beat down on Money Creek, baking it in the sun, Cal felt chilled to the marrow. "Did you know?" The words ground out of his throat. "About Maggie?" Just saying her name hurt.

Jack leaned on the wall across from Cal's cell and nursed his tin cup. "No. Powers didn't either until just recently. He was bragging that Marshal Maxwell had snuck back into town to meet him and bring him in on the investigation. That was less than a week ago. Before the stage got robbed this last time. He met with Maxwell and Maggie late one night."

Jack had no idea how his words cranked the vise holding Cal's heart. Secret meetings with Powers and Maxwell in the middle of the night? Not the Maggie he knew. Bitterness coated his tongue, and not all from the coffee. Had he ever really known her? "Can you send a telegram for me?"

"Depends. Who you want it sent to? Powers might not like it."

"Trace McConnell. I want it sent to a U.S. deputy marshal. He can't balk at that. If he does, then go over to the judge's house and clear it with him." Frustration made Cal's words sharp, and Jack's eyes narrowed and his brow puckered. "I'm sorry, Jack. I know this isn't your fault. I don't mean to get

112

you into trouble with the sheriff, but I need to get word to Trace about what's happening."

"I won't be able to go until there's someone here to watch the jail."

"If you don't get it sent soon, I have a feeling it will be too late." Something in the last look Powers had directed at Cal had set a clock ticking in his head. He had a feeling his time might be running out.

Jack rubbed the back of his neck with his palm. "I'll see what I can do."

❧

Maggie stepped out of the telegraph office and shaded her eyes against the late afternoon sun. Sweat beaded at her temples, and she longed for a breeze to come by and cool things off. The air felt thick and heavy with moisture, and she wondered, if she could reach out and grab a handful and give it a squeeze, would water pour out.

"Pssst!"

Maggie scanned the street.

"Pssst! Over here." A dry whisper rasped from the alley between the telegraph office and Purdy's Mercantile. One long, bony finger beckoned her around the corner.

Her senses pricked, and she raised her knee, pulling aside her hem and reaching for the gun at her ankle as she peered around the corner.

Angus McConnell.

She relaxed and let her foot fall.

His bloodshot eyes and vein-cracked cheeks stood out in his gray face. Several days' worth of whiskers bristled on his hollow cheeks. He smelled of sweat, horse, and stale booze. His hand clawed hers and drew her off the street.

"Angus, what do you want?"

"Is it true? Did Powers arrest my boy? Word's all over town that Powers arrested him and you helped him do it."

Hunched as he was, his eyes were on the same level as hers, begging her to tell him something other than the truth.

"It's true. Stolen goods were found in Cal's room." The words tasted like ashes.

Angus tottered a bit and put his hand on the wall of the telegraph office to brace himself. "It's a put-up job. If the sheriff found something in Cal's room, then he put it there himself. He'd do anything to get one of us in jail."

"But he didn't plant the silver. It was in Cal's locked trunk, in a locked jewelry box. I picked both locks myself. Powers was there the whole time, but he couldn't have planted the evidence. I went with him directly from the jail. He had nothing in his hands."

"What was you doing with the likes of Powers?" His eyes narrowed to slits.

Maggie blew out a breath and contemplated the hill in the distance. "I'm an agent for the U.S. Marshal's office. I've been gathering information on the stage robberies that have happened in this area. In my job as an agent, I assisted local law enforcement with the execution of a search warrant." *And put the final nail in the coffin of my happily-ever-after.*

"An agent? Cal know anything about this?" Angus edged away, as if he thought she would arrest him.

"No, I couldn't tell anyone. Though your other son, Trace, knew. He wasn't happy about not telling Cal, but as it turned out, it was the right thing to do." As disappointed as she was, as hurt and disillusioned, Cal's family would be even more so. "I didn't want it to be true. I'm very sorry for the way things have turned out." Angus would never know how sorry.

He wiped the heel of his hand under his nose and shook his head. "I know my boy. He wouldn't steal. Not anymore. None of my boys would. Not cattle, not money, not so much as an extra biscuit off the counter at the café. No, ma'am. My boys aren't like me. They're better than me."

Though Maggie admired his loyalty, she couldn't believe the word of a drunken father over what she'd seen with her own eyes. "He's been in jail before. For stealing."

Angus brushed aside her words. "That was before, when he was a kid who didn't know better." He stood a little straighter. "Us McConnells might be a lot of things, but we ain't no liars. I'll wager Cal says he didn't do it, don't he?"

"That's what he says." Cal's defiant declaration of his innocence seared her memory, but it was the hurt, betrayed, bewildered look in his way-too-blue eyes that made her heart crumple. If she'd walked up and stuck him with a knife, she doubted he could've looked any more shocked and pained. She thrust those thoughts aside. *She* was the one who was shocked and pained. He'd betrayed *her* trust. He'd made her fall in love with him, when all along he was part of a crime spree, robbing and killing, terrorizing travelers. "He said he didn't do it."

"Uh-huh, then that's the truth. Cal's a God-fearing man, a good man, and he always tells the truth. If he says he didn't do it, then he didn't." He grabbed her wrist again, his eyes narrowed. "Why pick the lock on that trunk? He don't lock it. The key is always stuck in the lock."

She brushed off his hand. "It was locked. And there was no sign of a key. We searched the entire room."

"I'm telling you, he don't lock the trunk for the same reason he don't lock the door. He keeps both open in case I need a place to go or something to wear." He brushed his tattered shirt, pressing his lips together and breathing deeply through his nose. "Cal, he don't got a wife and kids. He just has me. He leaves his room open and that trunk unlocked for when I need something. He doesn't have any valuables there. He knows I'd take 'em and spend 'em on drink if he did. There's no way he would keep a fancy box and silver bars in that room."

The more he talked, the more Maggie wanted to believe

him. What Angus said lined up with the Cal she had thought she'd known, but she couldn't trust that. Could she? She'd been wrong too many times before. And yet, Cal wouldn't leave silver in his room where Angus could get his hands on it and go on a drunken spree. But if Cal didn't put the silver there, who did?

"I gotta get in to see Cal, find out what's going on." Angus scrubbed his whiskers.

"Maybe you'd best stay out of things. I wired Marshal Maxwell. He'll take over as soon as he gets back from Boise. As soon as the trial is over up there."

"I can't stay out of it. He's my son. I've been in Powers's jail before. The longer Cal is in there, the less I like my boy's chances of getting out."

"What do you mean?" She grabbed his arm this time. "He'll stay in jail until he stands trial."

"I mean it wouldn't surprise me at all if my boy got accidentally shot while trying to escape or something." Angus walked back two steps and sat on an upended crate. "Powers is a big fish in this little pond. He hates us McConnells. He hates Alec for marrying Clara. Alec is a big landowner around here. Powers has always wanted to be a big dog and bark at all the little dogs. Now Alec's a big dog. And that isn't a marker to how he hates my other boys."

"But why hate Cal? Or Trace? What can they possibly have done to Powers to make him feel that way?"

"Powers's envy's been gnawing on him like a rabid skunk ever since Trace got made a deputy marshal."

"But what about Cal?"

"They never were exactly what you would call cordial, but they fell out over a girl. The sheriff never got over it. Powers hates Cal because Cal is everything Powers ain't. He's likable and handsome and girls are taken with him. You've seen yourself how Cal sort of brings sunshine with him wherever he goes." Angus's mouth quirked up in a smile that showed his yellowed teeth. "Powers has about all the appeal of a day-old road apple. Folks tend to scatter when he shows up."

"Just because Powers doesn't like Cal doesn't mean he would frame him. What about the other evidence? Cal would be in a position to know when the Money Creek stage would be carrying substantial amounts of money. When the stage was held up, one of the robbers not only knew him by name but Cal called the robber by name as well. All of that might be considered circumstantial, but there's the fact that stolen goods from that very robbery were found in his possession."

Angus's shoulders sagged as she listed the points. "How did Cal explain knowing the outlaw by name? You did ask him about that, didn't you?"

She had, and at the time, she'd believed him, but she didn't know what to think anymore. Late last night, holding that silver bar in her hands, she'd been so overwhelmed, so sure of his guilt. Now, after seeing his face, seeing the faith his father had in him, her certainty wavered. "He said he recognized the outlaw's horse, and that he'd chased the man before when he and Trace were tracking the men who kidnapped Rose."

"Then that's the truth, and you can bank on it." He lifted his chin, the fire of belief shining in his eyes. "My son ain't guilty. I know it as sure as I'm standing here. I think, if you'll search your heart, you'll see I'm right, that you believe in his innocence, too. I'm not a fool, though there's some who would say I am. I see more than folks give me credit for, and one thing I've seen is how much you love my son and how much he loves you. I've known it since I saw you together at the celebration on the Fourth. He couldn't take his eyes off you, and you bloomed like a rose every time he came near." A wistful expression flitted across his haggard face. "I remember feeling just that way when I met my wife."

Maggie's heart convulsed. She did love Cal. Otherwise his

arrest wouldn't hurt so very much. As for his love for her? "If Cal ever did love me, he surely won't after today."

❧

"God, what am I going to do?" Cal sat on the cell bunk, his back against the wall and his legs stretched out before him. He raised one knee and laid his hat on it. Scrubbing his hair with one hand, he squeezed his eyes shut then pressed his thumb and index finger against his eyelids. Anger licked at his insides, but his overwhelming emotion was sadness. She'd betrayed him. He'd trusted her. He'd loved her.

Images of her flashed in his head. Her laughing. Her prim little mouth tightening when she thought he was being outlandish. The gentle expression that came over her face when she held Rose. Her pitching in and rolling out pie crusts. Her marching down the street carrying that big suitcase. The way she fingered that odd necklace that had been her father's watch chain. A hundred different memories, and every one of them shrouded in falsehood.

How could he be in love with her when everything she'd told him about herself was a lie? An agent for the U.S. marshals? How did Trace figure into this? Had his brother known of her real identity? If so, why hadn't he told Cal? And the evidence they'd found in Cal's room, how had it gotten there? And why? Why would anyone want to frame Cal for the robberies? Who hated him that much?

The heavy door separating the cells from the front office rocked back. Powers filled the doorway. "I always knew I'd have you back in here someday." He stuck his thumbs behind his suspenders. "Not much has changed, has it?"

Cal swung his legs off the bunk and stood, taking his time replacing his hat. His stomach muscles clenched. Powers's nasty sneer made his skin crawl.

"No, you haven't changed a bit." Cal put plenty of meaning behind his words. "I don't belong in here, and you know it.

I won't be in here long, not once my brothers and the colonel come." He prayed they were on their way even now. Surely, between the three of them, they could figure a way to get him out of here, even if only on bail. Then he could start trying to figure out who had framed him and why.

With each heavy step Powers took toward the bars, the keys on his belt jangled. "I wouldn't put too much trust in them. You're caught, dead to rights. There isn't anything your brothers can do to change the fact that the evidence ties you straight to the robberies. You'll sit in that cell until the trial, then swing. A quick drop and a sudden stop for you." His chest expanded. "I can see the headlines now: LOCAL SHERIFF CRACKS CRIME RING THAT BAFFLED U.S. MARSHALS FOR MONTHS." With one beefy hand he framed each word in the air. "Then we'll see who people look up to and respect around here."

Cal clenched his fists. "Is that what this is? A grab for glory? A chance to look good? How much respect will folks give you when they find out you jailed the wrong man?"

"I didn't jail the wrong man. The right man is finally in a cell where he belongs." Powers approached the bars. "You've been running maverick too long. It gives me a heap of pleasure to see you standing in there. And"—he chuckled— "to know it was a woman that put you there." He threw his head back and laughed. "You've had every filly in the territory chasing you, and what happens? You fall for Maggie Davis, who was leading you on from the start. If it wasn't for her, we never would've tied you to the crimes. She played you like a fiddle, and you danced like a trained bear."

A sledgehammer couldn't have done more damage to Cal's pride. Every word was a heavy blow. Each one hurt all the more because Powers was right. She'd led him on from the start, and he'd followed after her like a hound dog on the scent of fresh bacon.

❧

An hour before dinnertime, the Rusty Bucket was deserted. Except for Georgia, who wiped the front counter with a wet rag.

The yeasty smell of bread and the fruity smell of pies wrapped around Maggie, but she couldn't raise any enthusiasm for food. She sank down at a table by the window.

The look Georgia gave her wrenched her already tangled feelings. The news must've spread to the café. Of course Georgia, Cal's biggest champion, would be upset.

Georgia didn't hesitate. She slapped the rag onto the counter and barreled across the café. "What were you thinking?" Her fists jammed onto her rounded hips and her brows slammed down toward her nose. "Cal McConnell is no more guilty of robbing stages than I am."

Maggie placed her hands flat on the table and drew a shaky breath. "Georgia, please—"

"Don't you 'please' me, Maggie Davis. How could you do this to Cal? After all I told you about him. After all the time you've spent with him and after the fine way he's treated you, how could you turn on him like this? You played your part just fine. You let him get close to you, fall in love with you, and the minute you had him on the hook, you trump up some charges and have him hauled off to jail."

Maggie stood up, knocking her chair backward into another table. "How could *I* do this to *him*? What about what *he* did to *me*? You're awfully quick to jump to his defense, but have you stopped to think that maybe I wasn't playing a part when I fell in love with him? I didn't trump up charges. I was there when the stage robber called Cal by name. That was enough evidence for a judge to sign a warrant to search his room. I was also there when the stolen goods were found in Cal's locked trunk at the foot of his own bed." She aimed a finger at the ceiling. "They were upstairs in this very building, and there wasn't a thing I could do about it. I'm bound by the law."

Georgia froze for an instant then shook her head. "That's impossible." She pursed her lips. "Something don't add up."

"I wish it didn't add up, but everything points to his guilt." Maggie's shoulders sagged. "You don't know how much I wish things were different."

Georgia pointed to Maggie's chair. "Sit. I'll get us some coffee. There's something amiss here, and I want to hear every detail. When it comes to Cal, you know what you know and I know what I know, but I think we'd best all know it together."

On that convoluted note, she turned and headed to the front door. With a brisk click and flap, she locked it and turned the sign in the front window to say CLOSED. "There. Now we won't be disturbed."

Returning with hot coffee, she lowered her bulk into a chair and plunked her elbows on the table, resting her chin in her palms. "Now, start talking."

Maggie told Georgia about her job as an investigator, and about the stage being robbed and Hack conversing with Cal. "Cal explained how this Hack fellow knew him, and vice versa, and it sounded good, too. But when I told the sheriff about the robbery—which I had to do since he's in on the investigation now—and I told him Cal's explanation for things, he said we had to take the information to a judge, that it was just the link we'd been looking for. The more he talked, the more sure I was that if we just searched Cal's room we'd find nothing and Cal would be cleared."

Georgia shook her head. "Powers would do anything to get Cal in jail. He hates him. Ever since—" She broke off and studied the depths of her coffee cup.

"Ever since what?"

"Powers was in love with a young woman who lived here

a couple years ago—a friend of mine—Gladys Sheppard. Gladys came to Money Creek to teach at the school, and from the minute she arrived, Powers wouldn't leave her alone. She told me he made her flesh crawl. He waited for her every day to come out of school, hung around the boardinghouse, and showed up all over town, wherever she happened to be. He begged her to marry him. Finally, she told him she could never love him, that she loved someone else. He forced her to tell him who it was. She said it was Cal McConnell." Georgia shook her head. "She didn't love Cal. His was the first name that popped into her head. She thought by telling Powers she loved someone else he'd leave her alone for good."

"Did it work?"

"No. If anything, it made him worse. Not only did he not stop pressing Gladys, but he started making things difficult for Cal, spreading bad talk about him around town. Never letting Cal forget his rough past and the fact that Powers had arrested him before."

"What happened with Gladys? I don't think I've met her."

"You wouldn't. Gladys up and left town almost two years ago. Didn't even say good-bye. Just packed her things and took off. I guess she couldn't stand it anymore." Georgia twisted her coffee cup in her chapped hands. "I don't think Cal ever knew why Powers hated him so much. Gladys felt so bad about using him that way, but she was too scared to fess up. I never told him, because what good would it do?" She shoved her cup aside. "But enough about the past. Tell me what happened when you searched Cal's room."

Maggie went through every step, reliving the tension and feeling afresh the pain of discovering the silver in that trunk. "I picked the lock on the trunk then the lock on the jewelry box. The silver was in there, clearly marked with the Henderson stamp."

Georgia sat still for a long moment, staring over Maggie's

shoulder. "Something's wrong with that story."

"I told it just as it happened. I don't like the outcome any more than you do, but it's the truth."

"No, I'm not doubting what you're saying. I'm telling you that there's no way that Cal put that silver in a jewelry box and locked it in that trunk."

"Angus said Cal doesn't keep any valuables in that room."

"And for good reason. We went round about Cal leaving the door unlocked when he first started renting that room—though I can understand his reasons. I used to store extra supplies up there, but we moved them all out so they didn't get stolen, since he wouldn't lock his father out. I've seen that trunk a hundred times. The key is kept in the lock. Cal sure wouldn't leave a box of silver in that room. If he did, Angus would sniff it out and swipe it faster'n you can say sweet potato pie. He'd buy enough liquor to stun an ox and be drunk from now until Christmas. No sirree, that silver was planted there by someone who wanted to get Cal in trouble. And that someone is Sheriff Albert Powers or I'll eat my apron." The apron in question—a bright red affair with yellow stripes—clashed gloriously with Georgia's orange hair and just about everything else in sight.

"But how? The only time he was out of my sight was to get the judge. . .to sign the warrant." She closed her eyes, reliving every second of last night.

"Powers is a slippery snake. I wouldn't put it past him to have snuck into Cal's room with that jewelry box and silver and lock it in the trunk, then hurry back to you with the warrant."

Maggie fingered her necklace then grabbed it in her fist, squeezing until the links bit into her palm. "If what we're surmising is true, Albert Powers is up to his eyebrows in this robbery ring. He isn't just framing Cal but covering up his own involvement. How else would he have possession of the stolen goods to plant in Cal's room?"

A shadow passed by the window. Several shadows.

Maggie glanced out. A group of about a dozen men strode up the street toward the jail. Every last one of them was armed and wore a bandana pulled up over the lower half of his face.

Georgia heaved herself up. "That has all the earmarks of a lynch mob!"

thirteen

Cal raised his head at the sound of voices outside then dropped it again to contemplate the cracks between the floorboards once more.

Jack stepped away from the wooden filing cabinet and slammed the top drawer. A couple years Cal's junior, Jack was green as grass when it came to being a lawman. Up till now, Cal had considered him a friend. He went to the window and peered out. "Mess of people coming up the street. Maybe a dozen or so men."

"Hmm." Who cared about the comings and goings of the town?

"Cal." Something in Jack's voice made Cal look up again. "They're wearing kerchiefs over their faces, and every last one of them is carrying a gun."

Cal's mouth went dry. He eased to his feet and approached the bars. Slipping his hands around the cold, metal rods, he gripped them. "Jack, where's Powers? And Kane?"

"Sheriff went up the street awhile ago. Should be coming anytime now. He sent Kane to Boise on some business or other a few days ago. They didn't tell me what it was, and I've learned not to ask. Sheriff don't like folks knowing his business too much." Jack shifted his weight. "Those men aren't stopping. What do you suppose they want?"

"Me." Cal's mouth went dry.

Jack's eyes went wide. "What should I do?"

❧

Maggie ran up the street, but by the time she got there, the group had ranged into a half circle around the front porch of the jail.

The young deputy, Jack, stood in front of the door with a shotgun in his hands. "Y'all need to stay back." His voice wavered, and his Adam's apple lurched. He splayed his fingers then renewed his grip on the gun.

"Run that boy out here. We got a necktie waiting for him." One man brandished a rope.

"I can't let you have him. He's going to stand trial."

"If you don't hand him over, you'll be strung up next to him." The mob advanced another step.

The half circle tightened, and Jack backed up a step. Maggie's heart thudded. They had him on the run, and the standoff hadn't lasted a full minute yet.

She bent at the waist and lifted her hem to withdraw her derringer from the holster just above her shoe top. She hid the gun in the folds of her skirt and edged along the front of the saloon next door. Best not to let them know her intentions until she was in a better position.

Georgia marched across the street and elbowed a couple of men out of her way. "If you want Cal McConnell, you'll have to go through me." She crossed her arms and glared hard enough to bend railroad spikes. "You there." She jabbed her finger at the man in the center of the arc. "That you, Lyman Carstairs? You think you can hide behind that hankie?" Her gaze raked them over again. "And Reginald Moore, and Devlin Leighton? I recognize your voices. What would your wives say? Do they know you're here?"

A couple of the men shuffled their feet, but the one Georgia had called Lyman braced his legs wide and turned his shotgun toward the jail. "Get out of the way, you buffalo heifer. Henry Billington was my friend, and Cal McConnell had a hand in killing him and burning that stage, whether he pulled the trigger or lit the match himself or not. I aim to see he pays for it."

Maggie prayed they'd keep their focus on Georgia and that she'd keep them talking. She just needed a few more seconds to get into position. She stepped off the boardwalk and onto the street, moving slowly but steadily around the men.

The deputy nudged Georgia. "Ma'am, I appreciate the help, and I'm sure Cal does, too, but you ain't armed, and these fellows don't seem to care that you're a lady. I think you'd best get on back." He swallowed hard again, and his chest rose and fell in shallow jerks. "I sure do wish the sheriff would show up. Where do you reckon he is?" Jack's eyes tried to scan the street and stay focused on the angry men in front of him.

Lyman stepped closer. "Stand aside, or we'll have to drop you right there. You can't take us all."

Maggie took a couple quick steps to close the distance, cocked her pistol, and pressed it to the base of Lyman's neck. "I don't have to shoot all of you, just you." Her hand stayed rock steady, though her heart thundered in her ears. She'd never actually had to shoot a man before, and she prayed this wasn't going to be the first. The derringer might not have much stopping power, but under these circumstances it would get the job done.

"Who are you?" Lyman's voice went hoarse.

"Does it matter? I'm the one holding a gun to your head. Now, I want you to call these men off."

"No, we want McConnell. He killed my friend." The man's voice shook as did his hands on his gun.

"That's for the court to decide, not you." She rotated the barrel of the gun slightly against his skin to remind him of his predicament. "I want you men," she raised her voice, "to walk to the porch one at a time and lay your weapon down. Then back up across the street. Get over there on the mercantile porch where I can see you." She stared at the deputy. "Go inside the jail and bar the door. Don't open it until I tell you to."

"Maybe I better stay here."

"I appreciate the gesture, but your place is inside the jail guarding the prisoner. Maxwell or Trace would tell you the same." Even if her growing suspicions of Powers were unfounded and Cal did prove to be somehow involved in these robberies, she couldn't stand by and see him lynched.

The deputy went into the jail. The door thumped closed, and the sound of a crossbar dropping into place reached her.

Frustrated rage rippled from Lyman in waves Maggie could almost feel. "Drop your gun in the dirt and call your men off."

"I ain't leaving empty-handed."

"If you make me shoot you, you won't be leaving at all. I don't want to kill you, but I will if I have to. Then it won't matter what your men do. Please, call them off." How had a lynch mob formed so quickly? Most of the folks she'd met seemed to like Cal well enough, but here were a dozen men ready to string him up.

His hands shook. With a clatter, his gun hit the dirt. "Do it, men."

Hoofbeats thudded on the road, and Maggie dared a glance over her shoulder to assess this new threat. Relief swamped her when she recognized Cal's brother, Alec, and behind him, Colonel Bainbridge and Seb Lewis. Alec slid from his horse and jerked his rifle from his scabbard.

"Good to see you, Alec." Maggie moistened her dry lips. "These gentlemen were just about to put down their weapons and back off."

Alec's brown eyes glared hard, and the set of his jaw boded no good for anyone.

The colonel, wearing a gun on his hip but not drawing it, joined him on the porch at a more sedate pace. His appearance seemed to send a current through those present.

Seb hopped up on the porch beside Georgia. "I'll have you men know, I don't take kindly to you pointing guns at my bride-to-be." The little rancher's face contorted with anger. "You lower them shooting irons right now, or I'm going to start perforating some hides."

A man on the right side of the group slowly stepped toward the porch and laid his weapon down.

Georgia sprang forward, yanked the bandana down. She grabbed the man's hat and slapped the side of his head with it. "If you didn't know you were doing something wrong, then why try to hide your face? I want every last one of you to take off those cowardly masks, or I'll do it for you. You should all be ashamed of yourselves."

The men looked from one to the other. Then slowly, one by one, they tugged the half-concealing fabric down around their throats. With sheepish steps, each man approached the porch and laid his gun on the boards. They grouped together in front of the mercantile, shifting from foot to foot and looking at each other out of the corners of their eyes.

Sheriff Powers strode down the street from the direction of his home. "What is all this? Alec McConnell, what do you mean holding a gun on one of my citizens? Miss Davis? What are you doing?"

Alec kept his gun trained right on Lyman's gut. "Your *citizens* formed a lynch mob and tried to break into the jail to hang my brother." He waved toward the group. "These fellows were just leaving though."

They faded away until only Lyman and Maggie stood in the street.

Maggie withdrew her gun and eased the hammer down. The knot between her shoulder blades loosened. For some strange reason, her knees began to knock. But with careful steps, she made it to the porch.

❧

Cal strained to hear what was happening outside. When Jack, white faced and shaking, came back into the jail and barred the door, a couple of wildcats started up writhing in Cal's gut. "What's going on?"

"She's got them strung up between the tail and the snoot." Jack leaned against the wall and eased the shutter aside to peek out. "Twelve grown men, and she's backing them down."

"Who?"

"That little Maggie Davis. Walked right up behind Lyman Carstairs and put a gun to his head."

Cal's hands shook on the bars. What did she think she was doing out there? A mere slip of a woman against twelve armed men? His helplessness increased tenfold.

God, protect her. I don't want to see her get hurt, no matter what she's done.

"Riders coming." Jack opened the shutter another couple of inches. "It's your brother and the colonel."

The relief in his voice mirrored the relief coursing through Cal. Alec and the colonel would sort things out. His breath lurched under his ribs and staggered out of his throat. He could almost feel the noose dropping off his shoulders.

"The men are laying down their guns and walking away. Georgia's making them take off their masks. Hey, I know that fellow. He works at the Red Eagle Mine. And that's Buck. He works on the Givens place as a cowhand."

Cal eased back down onto the bunk and hung his head. People he would've thought were his friends, or at least not his enemies, and they'd come looking to kill him.

"Sheriff's here. Just coming up the street now."

"He's a bit on the late side."

A fist thumped the door. "Jack, open this door right now."

The deputy made short work of letting them in. Powers strode across the room, brow like a thundercloud and eyes snapping. "How did you let this happen?" He rounded on Jack. "I turn my back for less than an hour, and there's a standoff at the jail?"

Alec laid his rifle on the desk and edged into the hallway in front of the cells. "Cal, you all right?"

Cal nodded and stood to go to the bars.

"Stay back." Powers motioned Alec away from the cell door. "You can talk, but you don't need to be close to do it. Alec, keep your back to the wall there. You, McConnell, stay away from those bars."

"Cal, what happened? Why's he got you in jail?" The colonel advanced to stand next to Alec, but Powers didn't bark at him the way he had at Alec.

Cal opened his mouth to spill the whole story when Maggie entered the jail. His throat dried up, and his heart shriveled. His beautiful betrayer. "I've got nothing to say with her here."

Her wide eyes shone wet, as if she fought tears, but he refused to be moved. He'd given her his heart, and she'd handed it back to him with a knife in it. She turned away from him and bent to stow a gun under her hem. The action, so foreign to the woman he had thought he'd known, just showed the chasm between his perception and reality. She was a stranger and a mystery.

She straightened and smoothed her hair. "I'll go then, so you can talk with your family. But I want you to know, Cal McConnell, that I'm not finished investigating, and the truth will come out. *All* of the truth."

He turned his back, amazed that she still had the power to hurt him when he was sure his heart was dead.

fourteen

"We've got to do something, but what?" Maggie paced the café dining room, weaving around tables and chairs.

Alec leaned against the wall near the hat rack and glared at her.

"You can stop that glaring, Alec McConnell. I know your brother is angry with me, but I can't help that right now." If only Maxwell were here so she could discuss the case with him. Everything kept circling back to Powers, but she had no hard proof. His grudge against Cal provided plenty of motive, and his position as sheriff meant he would be privy to information regarding silver shipments, especially since Hecker seemed to trust him. Was Hecker involved, too?

Georgia bent over a table, scrubbing the already-clean surface. "Whatever you're going to do, you'd best do it quickly, because if our hunch is correct and Powers *is* somehow involved in this whole thing, Cal won't last in his jail very long."

"With the colonel there, Powers can't do anything." Alec kicked a chair away from a table and straddled it.

Seb Lewis stood near the door, his rifle propped on his hip, and watched the street through the screen. "Nobody's moving out there." He mopped his face with a tattered, red bandana. "Sure wish this weather would break. Hot enough to roast a lizard in the shade."

Maggie's hair clung to her temples, and she fanned the collar of her shirt. "Someone needs to gallop up to Boise and fetch Maxwell and Trace back here. There's been no reply to my telegram, so we have to assume they didn't get it. Powers might have control of the telegraph office here, too." Maggie whirled. "Alec, you'll have to go. I can't, and I don't trust anyone else."

"I'm surprised you trust me." His dry inflection made her flinch. "From what Cal says, you don't trust anyone, especially not a McConnell."

"I don't have time to argue with you. Let me write a note to Maxwell, then get on your horse and ride."

Georgia fetched a pencil and paper for her.

Maggie scrawled a message, stressing the need for Maxwell to come quickly.

Alec settled his hat on his head. "Seb, I need you to do me a favor. I want you to take Lily and Rose and Georgia here out to the ranch. With Powers on the warpath and some townsmen set against Cal, I don't want that anger spilling over on Lily and Rose. Clara's alone at the ranch house with the baby. She needs some help. I'd be obliged to you both if you could look after my family until we get this settled."

Seb scratched his bristly chin and nodded. "We'll do it, won't we, Georgia?"

Georgia left off cleaning and went to Seb, who wrapped his arm around her waist and hugged her tight. "Don't you worry, Alec. We'll look after them. I'd best go pack some things."

Seb's eyes followed her until she left the room.

"You've got a treasure there, Seb. Don't let her go." Alec rose and shook Seb's hand. "I'm in your debt."

"Forget it. You'd do the same for me. Wouldn't be no use trying to keep Georgia from helping out somehow, and I'd rather have her safe at the ranch, too."

Maggie creased the paper and sat back. Alec was wise to get his family out of town. Before today's scuffle, she wouldn't have imagined such ill will existed in Money Creek, but situations like this seemed to divide folks, bringing out the best in some and the worst in others.

Alec took the paper from Maggie. "I'd like it if you went with them to the ranch. It would be the safest place for you."

She blinked and looked up at him. "No, thank you. My job is here."

"Your *job* is done. There's an innocent man in jail because of you. I don't think Cal will survive much more of you doing your job."

Maggie turned her lips inward and bit down, bowing her head for a moment and taking a deep breath until the pain of his words receded enough for her to speak. Then she stood. "I know you have no reason to believe me, but you'll never know how sorry I am that I didn't trust Cal. My only defense is that faced with what seemed like overwhelming evidence I faltered in my belief in him. The truth is, for the first time in a long time, I allowed myself to trust, to believe someone when he said he loved me. You don't know how hard that was. When I saw the stolen silver, I jumped to the conclusion that Cal had lied to me the same way I'd been lied to before. I thought it was just another example of how faulty my judgment was."

Alec's stance relaxed, and he raised his hand in an apologetic arc. "Maggie, I can see how it might've looked. . ."

She gripped the edge of the table. "I'm convinced that someone is framing Cal. From what Georgia has told me, Powers had the motive and possibly the opportunity, but I need something solid to tie him to the outlaws. He must be involved with them somehow in order to have had the silver and the jewelry box to plant in Cal's room. Until I have that connection linking the sheriff and the outlaws, it will merely be Cal's word against Powers's as to how the stolen goods got into Cal's room."

Alec's expression softened. "You really do care about him? And you think you can find a way to link Powers to the crimes?"

"I have no choice. Unless I do, Cal could hang for murder."
Her heart quailed at the thought.

&

The colonel suggested yet another game of chess to the
sheriff, and Cal narrowed his eyes, tilting his head to see into
the office.

For the past three hours, Colonel Bainbridge had taken
up space beside the sheriff's desk, shooting the breeze and
acting like he had nothing but time to kill. Several times
Powers suggested that they both had things to do and hadn't
the colonel best see to them, but each time the colonel
ignored him.

And Cal suspected why.

Boots clomped on the boards outside the door.

The colonel's hand went to his gun, and Powers stiffened.

"It's me, Sheriff, with a prisoner." Jack's muffled voice came
through the door.

Powers lurched up and went to let them in.

Cal edged to the corner of his cell so he could look out
into the office. The sight of the prisoner made his gut churn.

Angus McConnell hung from Jack's grip, and with every
step, he took a wild, ineffective swing at the deputy. "I'm not
drunk, you louse! Lemme go! I ain't even shtarted drinkin'
yet. Not by a long shot. And that no-good bartender at the
Golden Shlipper had no call to throw me out. I was just
singing. Ain't no law agin singing, is there?"

"Calm down, Angus. You've had a skinful by the smell of
you. You'd best sleep it off." Jack dragged him toward the
cells.

Powers rocked on his heels, his thumbs tucked behind his
suspenders. "Place is getting littered up with McConnells.
Pack of criminals."

Angus jabbed his boot out as he went past Powers and
connected with the lawman's shin, then fell into the colonel's

lap and sprawled on the floor.

Powers yelped and hopped on one foot, holding his leg and glowering. "Lock him up, and if he won't shut up, cuff him to the bars." He snatched Angus upright and slapped him across the face, then shoved him back toward the deputy.

Angus went limp in Jack's grasp and sniveled, swiping his nose with the side of his hand. "I don't know why you're always pickin' on me. I ain't done you any wrong. My boy's in jail. If that ain't a reason to drink, I don't know what is."

Cal gripped the bars of his cell so hard his forearms shook.

Jack half carried Angus to the remaining empty cell and got him to the bunk. He flopped on the rough, wool blankets and closed his eyes. Jack shook his head and shot Cal an "I'm sorry" glance. The metal door clanged shut on Angus, who seemed not to hear.

"Close that dividing door. I don't want to have to listen to a drunk snore." Powers didn't wait for Jack to obey. He limped across the office and slammed the heavy door so fast Jack had to hop to get out of the way.

Darkness shut them in the cells. The only light came from a narrow slit window near the ceiling. Barely enough, in this late afternoon on the east side of the building, for Cal to make out the uneven shape that was his father in the next cell. His rhythmic snores rasped on Cal's frayed nerves.

Then they stopped.

Cal's blood chilled. He knelt on his bunk and grabbed the bars of the dividing wall between the cells. "Pa, you all right? That slap didn't hurt you, did it?"

A chuckle came through the gloom. "Naw, that little tap, that ain't nothing compared to some of the licks Powers has given me through the years."

The clarity of his voice stunned Cal. "Pa?"

Again Angus chuckled and swung his feet over the side of the bunk. "Thought I was drunk, didn't you?" He stood and crossed the cell, which only took two steps. "Naw, it was all an act. I had to get in to see you, and I knew our beloved sheriff wouldn't go for that. He'd rather feed me a cup of cold poison than do me a good turn. I come to help you." His gray face appeared lighter in the gloom than his dirty brown jacket.

"Well, that's nice, but how are you going to help me when we're both stuck in jail? Did that little fact escape your attention? Or are you putting me on about being drunk? You smell like the bottom of a whiskey keg."

"That was all part of the plan. I had to dump some whiskey on my clothes and then cause a ruckus in the Golden Slipper so I could get arrested. I spilled about six beers when I staggered into a table of miners having a drink. Made a terrific mess. The bartender howled like a pitchforked bobcat. Then I started in singing. Bawdiest ballad I could think of. Wasn't more than a couple of minutes before Jack collared me and hauled me down here."

"Wonderful. Yet another heartwarming McConnell memory for the people of Money Creek." Cal paused. "You said plan. Your plan or Alec's plan? Did Alec send you here?"

"Naw, Alec went to Boise to get Trace. You're behind the times, son. Which is funny, because it's usually me that's behind. No sirree, the plan was Maggie's from start to finish. Well, except for the singing. I did that myself." His lips split in a ghoulish grin. "Kinda proud of that part."

Cal thrust away from the bars and went to lean on the far wall. "Maggie's plan. Then no thanks. What are you doing listening to her anyway? You can't trust her any more than you can fly. Getting you in jail was a stupid plan anyway. How is that supposed to help? Did she think I was pining for company?"

"Now, son, you haven't heard the whole plan." A tiny jangle of metal reached Cal's ears.

In spite of himself, he stepped forward to see what Angus held in his hands. Maggie's necklace. The one made from her father's watch chain. "She gave you that? What for?"

"Just watch."

Cal had to get closer and focus hard, but in just a few deft movements, the chain fell apart in Angus's hands.

"Lock picks." Angus brandished them like a fistful of horseshoe nails. "We're going to break out of jail." His smile broadened. "Maggie figured nobody would bother to search a drunk who lands in jail at least once a month and has never tried to escape before."

Cal wondered if he'd ever really known Maggie. Lock picks? What kind of girl carried a gun and a set of burglar's tools? "How are we supposed to get past Powers?"

"Easy." Angus made a dismissive wave. "Powers never spends the night down here. He's too soft for that. Jack minds the jail at night. Our sheriff will head home to his cozy bed. When I kicked Powers in the shin, I passed the colonel a note from Maggie. He'll leave at the same time as Powers. Jack won't be any trouble. He has no love for Powers, and once Maggie charmed him, he agreed to make a little trip to the outhouse after dark so's he won't be underfoot when we make our escape."

"Maggie charmed him?" Figured. "Well, forget it. I don't want any part of a plan hatched up by Maggie Davis."

"Don't be so thickheaded and stubborn. How long do you think it will be before another lynch mob rushes this jail? Maggie's only thinking about keeping you safe."

"Why?" Cal asked the question burning in his head and heart. "Why would Maggie do this?"

"She's got a few reasons. One, she's feeling guilty about not telling you she worked for the marshal. Two, because she believes you're innocent and Powers has something to do with the robberies. With you in his jail, if he *is* guilty, you're in danger. He can't take the chance that you'll be proven innocent, so he'll need to get rid of you. And there's a third reason."

A faint ray of hope shot through Cal's chest, but he smothered it with a ruthless jab. Maggie thought him innocent? That was too little, too late.

Angus continued. "I was in Purdy's store today when Powers came in and started talking about how this town shouldn't stand for you getting off, not when their own good men had been shot and burned and had died to protect the stage line. Though he never said they should come down here to haul you out and hang you, he prodded those men into a lynch mob. I followed him when he left Purdy's, and he went right to the Golden Slipper and stood a round for every man who agreed with him that McConnells were no-good thieves and drunks and killers and that the town would be better off without them. Then he disappeared. Went up to his house and waited for his plan to unfold. Sure enough, he found some numbskulls willing to do his dirty work." The entire time Angus talked, his fingers worked the probes in the lock on the other side of his cell door.

Cal had a renewed urge to get out of the jail. He found himself listening for the sounds of another mob. "Do you know how to use those things?"

"Maggie showed me, but it's harder when you can't see what you're doing. I'll manage it, but there's no hurry. We can't get out until we hear Powers leave anyway." Angus tried another probe. "Maggie's suffering, boy. Suffering something terrible. That's the third reason I mentioned that she's helping you. I think she loves you."

"She's got a funny way of showing it." Cal crossed his arms and leaned his shoulders against the bars. "She works for Powers, remember? You can't trust her. She made me fall in love with her, when the whole time, she was just trying to get enough evidence to arrest me. She's been lying to me all along, using me to get information. If that's love, then no thank you."

Angus snorted. "That's a bunch of hogwash. Maggie works for Maxwell, not Powers, and though she might've been bowled over by finding that stuff in your room, she's come to see you're innocent. If she didn't, then why would she risk her career to help you bust out of jail? Right this very minute she's gathering supplies and horses for us to get out of town until your brothers and Maxwell get back here from Boise. We'll camp out and wait, then ride into Money Creek and turn ourselves in. By that time, maybe Maggie will have turned up some evidence that will prove you didn't rob any stages." He shifted his weight so he could reach the lock better. "If you'd stop being sore and try to see things from her place, you'd maybe not be so hard on her. She's trying to make amends for doubting you."

Cal considered his father's words. How did one make amends for destroying trust? He couldn't trust Maggie, not when she'd lied to him about who she really was. Not when she'd used him to further her investigations.

Angus swung his door open. "For the first time, getting out of jail is going to be easier than getting in." He stepped into the open space in front of Cal's door and knelt. "This one should go faster."

In less than five minutes, he had the cell open. Cal started forward, but Angus waved him back. "Stay in there with the door pulled almost shut, just in case the sheriff decides to take a last look in." He followed his own advice and returned to his cell. The corn shuck mattress rustled as he lay down.

Cal paced, anxious to get on the move now. He'd rather be doing than thinking.

The sheriff's voice rumbled from the office.

"Man has a voice like a cranky grizzly."

Angus grunted. "Getting darker in here. Must be about sundown. Powers will be leaving soon." As Angus spoke, the front door opened and closed again. "There you go, just like we thought. Now we wait to give Powers a chance to get farther away and for Jack to do his part."

Time stretched out for Cal. He clenched and relaxed his hands. Boots scraped the floor on the far side of the door, and metal clanked. The heavy barrier opened a crack and stopped. A slice of lamplight split the cell area. Cal leaned away from it, staying in the dark. Then footsteps sounded, along with a tuneless whistle, and the front door opened and shut.

"There you go, just like we planned." Angus stepped into the light and pushed the door open to reveal the office. "Let's go."

Feeling like he was in a waking dream, Cal followed his father across the jail and outside.

❧

Maggie blew out a breath she didn't realize she held when Cal and Angus slipped out the front door of the jail and around the corner of the building into an alley. Her career working for the law slipped away with them into the dark. Aiding and abetting a suspected murderer. She pressed her palm to the wavy glass pane of the Rusty Bucket front window and swallowed against the lump in her throat. The list of charges that could be filed against her grew with every step Cal took away from that jail.

She wanted to go to him, but she wouldn't. Having played a role in getting him arrested and nearly lynched, too much stood between them. The best she could hope for was to uncover sufficient evidence to clear his name. . .then get away from Money Creek. As far away as possible.

fifteen

They barely got camp made before the weather broke. Cal edged back under the canvas overhang and lifted his collar around his ears. "Coming down like stair rods."

Angus sniffed and hunkered down beside him. "Wouldn't you know it?" He hiked his blanket up over his head and shoulders like a woman's shawl. "Rains every time I have to camp out."

"I'd rather be out here getting soaked than in that nice cozy jail." Cal spoke over the pounding of the rain. A waterfall streamed off the lowest point of the lean-to, obscuring the two horses tethered to a pine tree. "But I feel like we should be doing something instead of sitting here waiting."

"Like what? Maggie said to sit tight until she came to get us. That won't be for at least a couple of days yet, because it will take at least that long for Alec to get to Boise and back with Trace and Maxwell, especially in this weather. Good of Maggie and the colonel to get the gear together for us so we can wait out the storm in a little bit of comfort."

Thunder boomed and vibrated the ground under Cal's boots. "I ain't much for sitting still. I'd rather be out chasing Hack."

"Hack?"

"The fellow who robbed the stage. Robbed the Elko stage, too. He was in on the rustling last spring, and he also helped kidnap Rose last fall. I was this close"—Cal held up his finger and thumb a half-inch apart—"to catching him, but like an idiot, I let myself get thrown from my horse, and Hack got away." Disgust at himself roughened his voice. "If I ever catch up to him and his shaggy old pinto again, he won't get away."

"Shaggy pinto?" Angus went still.

"That's right. He rides a mean-looking black and white. I found his tracks near the burned-out carcass of the Elko stage. I didn't tell Powers. Figured I'd wait until I could talk it over with Trace and Maxwell." He picked up a stick and poked the mud.

Lightning forked, making the world glow phosphorous yellow and spring-grass green for an instant, quickly followed by roaring thunder that shook Cal to his core. Angus grabbed his arm. He shouted something, but the storm drowned it out.

When the noise faded away to just the splattering of the rain, Angus tried again. "A black-and-white pinto? Shaggy? And this fellow, he carry a bone-handled knife in his belt?"

"That's right." Cal's attention sharpened.

"And he helped kidnap my granddaughter?"

Cal blinked, unscrambling the thought. It was the first time he could remember Angus referring to Rose as his granddaughter. "That's right. He's a mean one."

Angus arranged the tarpaulin and sat down, cross-legged. "When I can't sleep, I usually take to walking around the town."

Exasperation formed a frown between Cal's eyebrows. "What are you talking about, Pa?" The words shot out before Cal could stop them. Those night rambles more often than not ended up in the Golden Slipper and someone banging on Cal's door to come get his pa before they had to roust the sheriff.

"I'm telling you I've seen that horse in town." A sort of exultant dread colored Angus's speech. "Last time I was in jail... well, before today"—he coughed and cleared his throat—"Trace and Maxwell were there. They thought I was passed out. The minute Powers stepped out, they started talking about the robberies and how they both thought there was some heavyweight pulling the strings, some boss behind the robberies and rustling and kidnapping. Both the girls, Clara and Lily, had heard talk when they'd been taken, talk of someone the rustlers and kidnappers were scared of."

"I remember, but they never heard who it was."

"You might ask the sheriff about that."

"What would Powers know?"

Angus tugged at his earlobe. "Maggie thinks Powers is behind all this. That he put the silver in your room. That he's been behind all the thieving from the beginning. I think so, too."

"Are you drunk?"

"Just roll the idea around a little. See what you come up with. What do you know about this boss?"

"All right. I'll humor you. We know the stage robberies started first. Over the past two years, fourteen stages in this corner of the territory have been robbed. None of the stolen property has been recovered."

"How much are we talking about?"

Cal shrugged. "All told? I've no idea, but more money than you or I will ever see. Cash, silver, gold. Mostly silver. That's where your reasoning falls down. If Powers was behind this, wouldn't he have some cash to flash? Why stick around here as a tin-pot sheriff when you're sitting on that kind of loot?"

"Maybe he's more canny than you think. Maybe he can't do without the petty power of being a sheriff. Maybe he is stealing because he can't help it, not because he wants the money. Or maybe he knows that the quickest way to get caught is to have more money than you're supposed to have."

Cal considered this for a while. "Trace figures the boss has been using the cash stolen from the robberies to pay off the men, and he's been stashing the silver and goods that could be easily identified until he can either get them out of the territory to be exchanged for cash or until he can leave the area himself with the loot."

"He's had a lot of men on the payroll, and you and Trace and Alec have dried up his ready sources of cash. The ranch and the cattle went to the colonel and Seb, and you and Trace busted up the kidnapping ring and got all the kids returned to their rightful homes."

"At which time these outlaws returned to robbing stages, but I don't see how you've tied this boss to Powers. It could be anyone."

"I'll tell you how. Because that shaggy pinto, and this Hack fellow with the big knife?" Angus leaned close. "I've seen that very horse tied up at night behind the sheriff's house on more than one occasion. Hack visits him at least twice a month."

Cal couldn't deny his pa a moment's triumph when he lobbed that bit of dynamite.

❧

Maggie wandered through Lily's empty house, heart-heavy and drifting. When she couldn't ignore the pain anymore, she prayed. "Lord, I'm lost here. I've been doing everything wrong. Cal's out there somewhere in this rain running for his life. Maxwell will fire me the minute he gets back to town. And rightly so. It feels like such a long time since I did anything right."

Thunder rattled the windowpanes, almost as if God were answering back. She hugged her upper arms and pressed her lips together to keep them from trembling.

I've been paying lip service to trusting God and not being afraid of what men can do to me, then turning back to do things my way. I've only thought about what others might do to harm me. I've let hurts of the past color my actions. Not ever laying aside the wrongs done to me. I've been carrying them around and pulling them out to go over and remind myself of how badly people have treated me, how I'm justified in being hurt and bitter and wary.

A hiccup lurched in her throat. "I judged Cal too harshly from the minute I met him. I distrusted him, and I allowed my hurt over Michael to cloud my thinking. I know Cal won't ever forgive me, but Lord, I'm asking You to forgive me and heal my heart. Help me to forgive hurts in the past and to trust You."

She bowed her head, and a tear slipped down her cheek. The image of Cal's pained, accusing glare the last time she'd seen him made her breath hitch. The sound of the cell door clanging shut on him would haunt her for the rest of her days. She'd broken his heart, thrust his love back at him, and allowed Powers to persuade her of his guilt.

Powers. He had an obsession about the McConnells and Cal in particular. He'd all but led a lynch mob to the jail to hang Cal. Was it just revenge for losing Gladys, or was it something else? If she was going to clear Cal's name, she'd have to do it herself. Before the sheriff caught up with him.

Boots clomped on the porch, and Maggie palmed her gun. She edged back the calico curtain to peer into the downpour. Relief made her knees weak. She holstered the gun and went to unlock the door.

Colonel Bainbridge entered the parlor. "Everything's quiet in town, and Cal and Angus got away clean. Powers blustered around the jailhouse for a while, but he's gone home now. Jack took a tongue-lashing from our sheriff that would make the devil himself squirm. That was some plan you came up with."

"Did Cal say anything?"

"Just thanked me, took the reins, and rode out. There wasn't much time for chatting."

The colonel smoothed his moustache and bent a sharp glance at her. "Might be a good idea if you got some sleep.

I'm going to head to Cal's room over the café for the night. Don't know if I'll sleep much, but I can keep watch from his window up there."

Knowing she wouldn't be able to sleep, she lit the lamp in the kitchen and spread all her case notes out on the tin-topped work surface. Every interview she'd written up, her description of the robbery, and the search of Cal's room. She bit her lip. Something tugged at the corner of her mind about that warrant. Powers had tucked it into his desk drawer. He should've given it to Cal, or at least left it in the room after their search was complete. Tension built, and she tried to ease it away by rubbing her forehead. She'd like a look at that warrant. Making one quick search of Lily's kitchen drawers, she found the implement she needed then hurried down the street to the jail.

Jack answered her knock. "Miss Davis." His eyebrows climbed. "You'd best not be here. Powers is on the warpath. I had to raise the alarm about Cal and Angus getting free." He grinned. "Powers is mad enough to spit shiny new nails."

"Colonel Bainbridge told me. I won't stay. I just need something from the sheriff's desk."

Jack shifted his weight. "Miss Davis, I've gone along with this about as far as I can. I don't know that I should let you do any more. If I hadn't seen that lynch mob with my own eyes, I'd never have let Cal and Angus go free. It was only your word that he'd turn himself in the minute the marshals got back that convinced me to help."

"Don't help me, just don't stop me. Please. I need to follow a hunch I have. It's nothing illegal, I promise. I just need to look over the evidence once more. You can even watch to make sure I don't do anything to tamper with the evidence."

The young deputy stepped back and gave her access to the desk. The drawer where Powers had stowed the silver was locked, as she expected. She took the ice pick she'd borrowed from Lily from her pocket and plucked a paper clip from the bowl on the desktop. The lock yielded under her probing, and she dragged it open.

The warrant lay on top of the jewelry box. With a flick, she snapped it open and scanned the words. A hot coal of anger began to burn in her middle, and the flames leaped higher with every breath.

"This warrant is all wrong. No judge in his right mind would word things this way. No wonder Powers wouldn't let me see it. He must've written it out himself while I waited at the jail."

"What are you going to do?" Jack tugged at his lower lip. "Whatever it is, don't you think you should wait for Maxwell and Trace?"

"There isn't time. The sooner I tie Powers to the robberies, the sooner Cal will be safe." She folded the paper and tucked it into her waistband. "First we'll go see the judge and get a legal warrant."

Maxwell's warning echoed in her head. *"Everything by the book, but get creative if you have to."*

"Then we'll see about getting into Powers's place."

sixteen

Cal crept through the underbrush and took up his post near Powers's house where he could watch both the front and side doors.

Angus poked him in the shoulder. "This is a bad idea, son. If we're found, we'll be back in jail before you can say jackrabbit."

"I aim to sit right here for as long as it takes for Hack to show up. He won't get away from me this time. When I do catch him, he'll tell me what I want to know about Powers." He glanced up. At least the rain had tapered off. Little windows in the cloud cover revealed an indigo sky studded with stars. "Odd that the sheriff isn't in bed yet. Maybe he's waiting up for Hack."

They'd watched and waited about an hour when Jack trotted up the street and rounded the house to knock on the front door.

"What's he up to?" Cal muttered under his breath.

"I think you'd best come," Jack's voice carried to them. "Somebody shoved this note under the door. Says he knows where Cal and Angus McConnell are hiding out, and he'll meet you at the livery stable to tell you where they are."

"At this time of night? Who was it?" Powers's door opened a crack. "You're so far outside my good graces, I wouldn't think you'd have the nerve to come knocking on my door at this hour."

"I don't know, but I figured you'd want to head up there to check it out." Jack stepped back.

Powers muttered something Cal couldn't catch, then

shouldered into a slicker, blew out the lamp, and headed up the street with his deputy. "Fine, but this better not take long."

Cal raised an eyebrow and looked over his shoulder at Angus who shrugged. Before Cal could decide what to do, someone else emerged from between the buildings and headed toward the side door. A female someone.

Angus sniffed and swiped at his nose. "Looks like Maggie. I didn't hear this part of the plan."

Seeing her, even from this distance, was like getting gut-kicked by a mule. What was she up to? She crouched beside the doorknob.

He started to rise, to go to her to tell her to stay away, lest she get caught, or somehow warn off Hack if he showed up, but Angus grabbed his arm with claw-like fingers. "Don't."

"But she'll ruin everything."

"Maybe not. Maggie's a bright little thing. She can put the pieces together as well as you can. Maybe she's tumbled to something we don't know about. Why don't you trust her to know what she's doing?"

The irony smote Cal so hard he could hardly stand it. Trust her? He clenched his fists when the door opened and she slipped inside.

Angus loosened his hold on Cal. "If what we think about Powers turns out to be true, then he planted that evidence there on purpose to fool Maggie and to convict you. Maggie now knows you're innocent, and she's doing her best to clear you. If I'd come across that silver, it sure would've knocked me for six, and I've known you all your life. I'm not saying I would've thought you guilty, but I might've been tempted."

Cal kept his eyes on the house, waiting for candlelight to show. Jack must be in on it, drawing Powers away from the house so Maggie could search it. The rain picked up again, streaming off Cal's hat brim and muffling sounds.

Powers appeared out of the downpour and headed toward the front porch. Jack dogged his steps, speaking loudly. "But maybe they're just late. Don't you think we should wait for whoever it is down at the livery?"

"Stop yelling. The whole thing was a hoax, somebody messing with us."

"But, Sheriff—"

"Enough. Get back to the jail. Though I don't know what good you'll be there. You let the McConnells walk right out. Good night!" Powers went into the house and slammed the door.

Cal's heart lodged in his throat. Maggie was still inside. He willed her to escape out the side door. When he couldn't stand the waiting any longer, he stood. He'd have to go after her.

Angus yanked him down and pointed to their left.

The shaggy pinto shambled out of the gloom, head down against the rain.

Hack.

‌　　　　　　　　　　　　🙚

Maggie shielded the small bull's-eye lantern with her hand, trying to keep the light from playing on the windowpanes just in case someone was watching. Where might Powers hide stolen silver? She opened cupboards and drawers in the kitchen, wrinkling her nose at the pile of dirty dishes in the washtub and the musty smell. "Not exactly house-proud, are you, Sheriff?" She ventured into the bedroom, a feeling of distaste and disgust creeping over her flesh. Powers wasn't just untidy, he was slovenly. The bureau gave up no treasure, nor the trunk under the window.

The parlor was bare except for a horsehair sofa and a straight-backed chair. A small table stood near the kitchen door and sported the only ornamentation in the room, an ugly two-handled vase in pinks and greens. The second bedroom held only a bed frame without a mattress. The rails gleamed dully in the lantern light. Despair clawed at her. She'd been wrong. He must have another hiding place. If he'd buried it somewhere in the countryside, they'd have a hard time finding it.

Voices out front froze her. Jack all but begging Powers to return to the livery. Frustration wiggled up her spine. If only she had more time. Perhaps she should just face Powers with the warrant, but she was alone, except for a deputy green as a pea.

"Get back to the jail where you're supposed to be and leave me in peace."

Scratch that. She was just alone.

Two steps from the door, her hand reaching out for it, hooves plopped in the mud outside. She caught sight of a rider through the blurry window, swathed in a slicker and obscured by rain, swinging off his horse by the back steps. She ducked and blew out the candle in her lantern, praying the smell would disperse quickly. The stark kitchen offered no place to hide. Powers at the front and a stranger at the back.

She inched backward, trying to be quiet, searching for somewhere to conceal herself. She scrabbled at her hem and grabbed her gun. As she withdrew it, her foot hit something on the floor. She glanced down. A metal ring and the faint outline of a cellar door. In an instant she knew where the evidence lay. She grasped the ring, heaved the door up, and all but fell down the steep steps. Her shoulder protested being used as a brake to keep the door from thumping and giving away her location. The pitch black closed around her. She huddled at the bottom of the stairs, listening, trying to calm her breathing.

The back door opened overhead and boots scudded across the gritty floor. "Powers? Where are you?"

Maggie tilted her head. That voice, she'd heard it before.

More footsteps. "Getting rid of that useless deputy of mine." Powers's voice rasped against Maggie's skin like sand. "That might be a good job for you, Hack. He'll be an easy kill. He deserves it for letting McConnell escape."

Hack! She gritted her teeth. In a pinch, she might've been able to take Powers on alone, but not against two of them and her trapped like a gopher in the cellar.

The footsteps and voices moved toward the front parlor.

Maggie pressed her hand to her chest. She had the evidence she needed. Powers and Hack together, plotting the murder of a deputy. But as long as she was here, she might as well take a look. With trembling fingers she set her gun on the bottom step and struck a match to light the lantern. She picked up her gun and tucked it in her waistband alongside the warrant. When she held the light up, her breath caught in her throat.

A wall of shelves lay on her right, laden with silver bars. Two Money Creek Stage Line express boxes sat on the floor beneath them. She opened the one closest to her to reveal packages of bank notes and pouches of coins. The musty, dank smell of the dirt-walled cellar invaded her lungs as she took a deep breath. The mother lode, right here under Sheriff Albert Powers's house. A box of watches and fobs, a silver cigar case, an amethyst pendant—valuables purloined from passengers and hoarded here like a squirrel saving up for winter. The jewelry box and silver bar Maggie had conveniently found in Cal's room must've come from this cache.

Her hands shook, making the light wobble and the shadows dance. She needed to get out of here, to tell someone what she'd found. One last corner lay in darkness. She raised her lantern and edged forward. Two valises sat side by side. She loosened the clasp on one and tipped it so the light shone inside. Schoolbooks? A curious shiver raced up her spine. She flipped open the cover of the top book.

The inscription read: Gladys Sheppard.

With dread, Maggie opened several others. Every last one of them belonged to the former schoolteacher. She opened the other valise. Clothing, personal effects. A locket inscribed with the initials G.S.

With trembling hands, Maggie closed the bags. Had Powers murdered the schoolteacher? What other reason could there be for her belongings to be here?

She swallowed hard. Maxwell would deal with all of this when he got here. Cal would be exonerated, and Powers would be stopped, but not until Maggie got out of here to tell them. She headed toward the steps. What she needed was for Jack to use his head and create another diversion so she could get out of here. Would he think of it, or was he too unseasoned?

Boots scraped again overhead, and wood creaked, like someone settling down in a chair. She doused the lantern, afraid the light would show through the cracks around the trapdoor, and drew her gun.

"What are you going to do about Cal McConnell? You'll have to kill him on sight, you know." The chair creaked again. Maggie could see Hack in her mind, leaning back, his knife handle jutting from his belt.

A stove lid rattled. "If he's smart, he's headed out of the territory by now, but he ain't smart." More banging. "I've been waiting for word from Kane up in Boise. I sent him up there to silence that witness, but I have to figure he failed. If Kruger talks, we're both in the soup. With McConnell in jail and Kruger dead, I thought I could pin the whole thing on Cal and get rid of him, but that's all gone to smash." The stove lid crashed down, making Maggie jump.

"I think it's time to shut things down and get out of here."

"No. I'm not leaving. I've worked too hard, and I won't be

run off by a McConnell. I can still salvage the situation."

"How?"

"Find Cal McConnell and kill him before this thing goes to trial. I can pin everything on him, and he won't be here to fight it."

"And if you can't find him?"

Something hit the wall and shattered. A coffee cup or plate?

"I'll burn that bridge when I get to it, but I think I should move the stash before morning. Things are getting a mite hot around here. Go down to the livery and get a wagon. There's too much stuff to move on horseback."

"The silver's here in the house?" Hack's voice went up.

"Take that look off your face." The ominous and unmistakable sound of a gun being cocked. "You'll help me load it, and you'll get your cut, but after that, I drive away alone. I'll find a new place to hide the silver then sneak back into town in time to raise a posse to go after McConnell."

Gooseflesh rippled along Maggie's arms and the back of her neck. The stash lay stacked all around her. The only light came from the tiny cracks around the trapdoor, barely discernable from the bottom of the cellar.

Lord, help me get out of here. I don't want to wind up like Gladys.

seventeen

"I can't wait here. She's in danger!" Cal's fierce whisper when he wanted to yell made his throat ache. Maggie had been in the house for far too long.

"You can't. If they've got her and you bust in there like a bull, they'll shoot her and you, too."

The side door opened, and Cal tensed. Hack slipped out. He hiked his collar up around his ears and ducked his head against the rain. Instead of getting on his horse, as Cal expected, he headed up the street. What should he do? Cal wanted Hack so bad his fingers itched, but he couldn't leave, not with Maggie still inside. He nudged Angus. "Follow him. See where he goes."

Angus slipped away into the downpour, and Cal ground his teeth, waiting for Maggie to appear, torn with indecision. Did she have that little gun she carried? Was she already dead? He hadn't heard any shooting, but the knife in Hack's belt worried him. What was Powers doing now? The light remained in the kitchen, but he couldn't see any movement. When he couldn't stand it anymore, when he knew he had to at least get close enough to peer into one of the windows, something touched his arm, making him nearly jump out of his skin.

"Shhh!" Trace tugged on Cal's slicker. "Come with me."

Heart thundering in his chest, Cal shook his head. "I can't leave. Maggie is in the house with the sheriff."

"I know. C'mon."

He had no choice but to follow, questions bombarding him every step of the way.

A group of men stood under the pines—Maxwell, Alec, Angus, Jack, and the colonel. Off to the side, Hack stood with his arms wrapped around a tree, neatly handcuffed.

Cal's jaw dropped.

"Not much time to explain." Maxwell nodded to Cal. "It will be dawn soon, and we'll have to move."

"I brought these for you, Cal." Jack held out Cal's sidearm and holster, taken from him at his arrest.

Cal settled the gun belt on his hip, removed the gun, and checked the load.

Maxwell handed a hat Cal recognized as Hack's, along with a slicker, to Angus. "You're going to drive the wagon. You're the only one of us small enough to be taken for Hack."

Angus donned the clothing.

"The goal is to get Powers out of the house quietly. I don't want to alarm him by storming the house. If he's got Maggie. . ." He tightened his jaw. "If she's still alive, he'll use her as a hostage."

The marshal continued to give orders. "Alec, you and the colonel get around the back of the house. I don't want him to escape that way. Trace and I will be around front. Jack, you're going to stay here and watch the prisoner. We'll bring him to the jail when Maggie's safe and the sheriff is in custody."

"What about me?" Cal braced himself for an argument.

"I want you in the back of the wagon. The idea will be for Angus to lure Powers out onto the porch. You pop up from the wagon bed, and Trace and I will close in on either side."

☙

Over Maggie's head, scrapes and thumps sounded, like someone was dragging a box across the floor. That made sense. Perhaps Powers was bringing the trunk from the bedroom to load it with treasure. He'd need something to carry the silver bars in.

The darkness pressed against her eyes. She longed for the

comfort of the lantern. What if he came down the steps with his own lantern and the light blinded her?

"Where is he? He should've been here by now." Powers's voice startled her.

It had seemed like a long time since Hack left, but she had no way of judging the time. Maggie's hand sweated on the pistol grip. She backed into the corner of the cellar near Gladys's bags and squatted. How she wished for a weapon with more stopping power than the derringer. With only two shots, and those of small caliber, she doubted she could bring the sheriff down if he rushed her. Would she be better off taking her chances against him before Hack returned? She'd have no chance at all against both of them.

"Finally." His footsteps moved toward the front of the house.

A chance to escape. Her heart leaped and her feet followed suit. She crossed the dirt floor and groped for the stairs. If only he would stay out of the kitchen long enough for her to get away. A sharp pain exploded through her shin. She'd barked it on one of the express boxes. Even while tears stung her eyes, she got her bearings and corrected her course. A cry of thankfulness lodged in her throat when her hand grazed the wooden steps.

The most dangerous moment would be when she lifted the trapdoor. She ascended the steps as fast as she quietly could and steeled herself. Should she ease it open and try to sneak out or throw it open and bolt for the door? Enough wavering. She renewed her grip on her pistol and braced her shoulder against the door.

"Hey, it took you long enough."

Maggie stopped cold.

❧

Cal lay in the back of the wagon, face up, getting pelted by rain. Soaked to the bone, he held his gun on his chest and rocked and bumped along like cargo. Angus must be hitting every mudhole in the street. The peak of Powers's house showed to Cal's right as Angus pulled the wagon to a stop.

"Hey, it took you long enough," the sheriff's grizzly-like voice rasped.

Cal could just make out the top of the front door, which only opened a sliver in the pre-dawn gloom.

Angus wrapped the reins around the brake handle and kept his head ducked deep into his upturned collar.

The door opened a few more inches. "Come help me load the stuff."

The wagon lurched when Angus clambered down the side and shook his head at Cal. Powers hadn't come out onto the porch like Maxwell had figured. Now what?

"Quit dawdling. It'll be light soon, and there's lots to move."

Angus moved around to the back of the wagon and took his time lowering the tailgate. He mouthed a question to Cal and shrugged. What did they do now?

"Take your time and see if he edges out to see what you're up to," Cal whispered, his head only inches from the end of the wagon. "When he does, holler. Then you hustle around the side of the house out of the field of fire."

Angus lowered his hat brim and fidgeted with the lynchpin and chain.

Every muscle tensed, Cal waited.

"Hack, let's go. Time's wasting."

"Now!" Angus yelled and dropped from sight.

Cal bolted up and aimed at the front door. "Hands up, Powers."

The sheriff hesitated only a fraction of a second before he jerked at his gun. Cal fired, and Powers lurched backwards, slamming the door. Another shot from Cal shattered the glass in the door. He ducked when a bullet thudded into the side of the wagon box.

"Give it up, Powers. You're surrounded." Maxwell's voice boomed from the corner of the house.

Cal dared a peek out the end of the wagon.

Angus crouched beside the house behind Trace and beckoned for Cal to join him.

Powers shot the wagon again, splintering a board near Cal's head.

Cal regretted his awkward position.

"That you, Maxwell?" Powers yelled.

"That's right. There's no way out, so why don't you put that gun down and come out. We know everything. We've arrested Hack and he split open like a sack of beans. It's over, Powers."

"No it ain't. It ain't over until Cal McConnell's dead." He pumped two more shots into the wagon. "I won't be bested by that cur. I've got him pinned down. A few more shots, and he's mine."

Bam! Bam! Wood splintered and scattered over Cal's chest.

Cal took a fresh grip on his gun. A couple more hits like that, and the side of this rickety wagon would look like a cheese grater. He'd have to holler to Maxwell and Trace to provide him some cover fire so he could get out of there. He drew in a breath to yell, when he heard a couple of pops and Powers bellow. He raised his head in time to see the front window explode outward.

❧

Maggie couldn't believe what she was hearing. Maxwell was here? And Cal? Her head spun. She eased open the trapdoor and let it rest on the kitchen floor behind her. The side door and escape stood only a few feet away.

"A few more shots, and he's mine."

She froze. *Lord, help me.* She couldn't leave him. She couldn't run away and let Powers shoot Cal. Treading lightly, she headed toward the parlor.

Powers crouched beside the window, his left arm hanging limp and streaming blood. His right held his Colt, and he aimed it through the window once more.

Again she wished for a sturdier pistol than the derringer, but she'd have to use what she had. Creeping closer, she picked up the ugly vase she'd seen earlier. "Put your hands up, Sheriff."

He spun, aiming his gun at her.

She squeezed off both shots.

He jerked and dropped his pistol, his crazed eyes going wide. An unearthly yell ricocheted through the room, and he lurched toward her.

When he got close, she swung the vase, hitting him in the face. Glass shards splintered around them, and pain shot through her arm at the impact.

Powers grabbed his eyes and staggered backward, emitting an eerie wail. He tripped on the edge of the rug and fell. His momentum carried him through the front window and out onto the porch where he lay still.

*

Cal leaped from the wagon and jumped onto the porch, keeping his gun on the sheriff. He whirled when the front door opened.

Maggie stepped out, a small gun in one hand and the handle of a pitcher or something in her other. She didn't say a word, just looked at Powers, then at Cal, and dropped what she held to cover her face with her hands.

People gathered around. Maxwell and Trace mounted the steps and squatted by the sheriff. "He's still alive. Somebody better go for the doc."

Angus took on the task and trotted away. The colonel and Alec came from around the back.

"Well done, Maggie."

When Maxwell spoke, Maggie lowered her hands. All

expression smoothed from her face, and she stooped to pick up her gun. She nodded to her boss. "The stolen goods are in the cellar under the kitchen."

Cal, who had been on the verge of going to her, stopped. She sounded so detached and professional.

Maxwell seemed to take this for granted. He nodded and entered the house, patting Maggie's shoulder as he brushed by her.

Cal tipped the spent shells from his gun and reloaded the chambers before returning the weapon to the holster at his side. All the while he tried to reconcile the Maggie he'd planned forever around with the woman who stood before him now. A professional agent. A cold, detached stranger. Who had saved his life and broken his heart.

eighteen

Maggie avoided dissolving into tears by clinging to her professionalism. Focusing on the details of the case, tying up loose ends, and doing everything by the book allowed her to keep her feelings at bay. She knew it wouldn't last forever, but the blanket of numbness that had wrapped around her when she'd stepped onto the porch after shooting the sheriff comforted her.

Powers lay under guard at the doctor's house, and Hack sat in the jail singing like a magpie.

Maxwell and Trace questioned Cal and Angus, took statements from Maggie, Jack, the colonel, and even Georgia. Pieces of the puzzle fell together quickly with Hack's information, leading to the arrest of the two men who helped him rob the last stage. Maxwell anticipated further arrests, but as the investigation widened, he was able to clear men like Mr. Hecker at the bank and Joe Williams at the stage office.

Hecker, shaken that his good friend, the sheriff, had been systematically robbing him blind, praised the U.S. marshals. The treasures from Powers's cellar lodged in the bank vault as evidence. Joe helped with the inventory of the goods, producing bills of lading and shipping orders and matching them against the confiscated loot.

And through it all, Maggie fought to remain cool and calm. She answered every question Maxwell put to her, wrote up her report, and didn't sleep well. Each time she closed her eyes, she dreamed she had been too late and Powers had succeeded in hanging Cal for robbery and murder. In the week it took to tidy up her part in the investigation, she encountered Cal several times, but he never spoke to her. His silence cut her deeply, but she couldn't really blame him after the way she'd hurt him.

Now she just had one more detail to see to. "You never told me how you got here so quickly from Boise." Maggie signed her name to the bottom of her statement and handed it to Maxwell, who tucked it into the ever-growing case file.

He tapped the papers together and laid them on the desk in the jail. "We were almost to Money Creek when we met up with Alec. That prisoner in Boise finally confessed that Powers was his boss and behind all the robberies. What clinched it for us was when one of Powers's deputies, Kane, showed up and tried to murder Kruger on the way from the jail to the courthouse." Maxwell shook his head. "He's up there awaiting trial for attempted murder. I'm sure we'll be able to pin a few more charges on him before we're through."

"Has anyone said anything about the missing schoolteacher, Gladys Sheppard?"

Her boss tipped back in his chair behind the desk in the jail. "Hack did." He jerked his thumb toward the cells. "The sheriff killed the girl when she wouldn't return his affections and left it up to Hack to dispose of the body. Hack told us where he buried her. I sent Jack and Trace up there to check out the story. If she's there, they'll bring her body back and see that she gets a proper burial in the town cemetery."

Maggie nodded. "That's fine." She knew she sounded cold and detached, but she had to. If she allowed herself to feel instead of think, she'd come apart and bawl like a lost calf.

"You did a good job here. I wrote up a report for your file." He grinned. "I've got our next assignment, if you're interested."

"I'm not." She took a letter from inside her coat. "I'm done with the agent business. Here's my resignation." She laid it on the desktop.

"Now, Maggie"—Maxwell sat upright in his chair—"I know this was a hard one, but you can't just quit. Why don't you let things cool down a little? Why don't you think about it a bit?" He scowled. "I can't do without my best agent."

"I have thought about it. I've done nothing *but* think about it." She stood. "You'll find someone to replace me. I just have to get out. I can't trust my instincts anymore, and without instincts an agent is done for."

"Where will you go? What will you do?"

"I don't know yet. Something will turn up. I might head to Denver for a while. I have a cousin there I haven't seen in a while."

Maxwell protested, argued, and badgered, finally telling her she should take some time off to get her head on straight, and when she was ready, she could contact him to come back to work.

With a heavy heart, Maggie packed her bags. She left the case of lingerie at the jail for Maxwell to deal with, along with a note explaining how he would need to take delivery of Mrs. Purdy's latest order and get it to her. The thought of her boss handing over women's undergarments to the formidable Mrs. Purdy gave Maggie her only smile in days. At least he could connect Mrs. Purdy with his sister and keep the orders going for each of them. A small enough positive thing in amongst all the harm Maggie had done.

She also left a note for Lily, apologizing for not being able to be truthful with her about everything up front and thanking her for her friendship and hospitality. Maggie would miss sweet Rose's smiles and Lily's warm, open friendship.

Georgia crushed Maggie to her apron front when Maggie went to the café to say good-bye. "Are you sure this is what you want?"

"This is best for everyone, Georgia." Maggie blinked hard

to stem her tears. "Please, take care, and be extra good to Cal."
She stumbled on his name, the lump in her throat swelling.
"Good-bye, Georgia. Thank you for everything."

"I can't help but think you're making a mistake, girl."

Maggie sighed. "If I am, I can just add it to the long list of
mistakes I've already made."

She escaped and boarded the Elko stage. The town faded
into the distance, and Maggie felt as if her heart had been
left behind as well. She'd come into their lives and done
irreparable damage. There were things she just couldn't fix.
She had to get away.

à.

"What do you mean she's gone?" Cal stood in Lily's parlor
with his hat in his hand. Alec and Trace came in behind him
carrying Lily's bags and Rose, fresh from their stay at the
ranch.

"I mean she's gone. As in not here. As in vanished. As in
she has packed her bags and departed on the stage." Lily held
out the note. "She says she can't stay, that she loves us all very
much, but she's done too much harm, and she's sorry."

"What are you going to do about it?" Alec tipped his head
and challenged Cal with his stare.

Trace put his arm around Lily. "You going to let her get
away?"

The fear that had coursed through Cal when Lily told
him Maggie was gone intensified. He couldn't lose her. He'd
battled his feelings for days, knowing she deserved forgiveness
for hiding her identity, and having to acknowledge that, faced
with the same circumstances, he would've acted exactly as
Maggie had. "When did she leave?" He jammed his hat on
his head.

"I don't know. I just found her note."

He was halfway down the street before he realized Alec
and Trace were with him. "What?" He kept on walking.

"We're going along to see you do things proper."

"I don't need a bunch of lookers-on."

Alec grinned, unrepentant. "Maybe not, but we're going all the same. I wouldn't miss this for the world."

"Me neither." Trace followed them into the livery, and they wasted no time saddling up. "Just where is it we're going?"

"I'm going to rob the stage." Cal swung into the saddle and kicked his mount into a gallop.

&

Maggie used up a third handkerchief and told herself to stop being so silly. But the tears leaking out of her eyes wouldn't stop.

Her traveling companions, three men, ignored her as best they could but cast her occasional worried or exasperated glances.

At the way station, she picked at her food, unable even then to stem the silent tears.

When they reboarded the coach, the man across from her, owner of the second handkerchief, finally sighed and put his hat down over his face so he wouldn't have to look at her.

They'd been back on the road less than an hour when the coach began to slow. Maggie sat up, dropping the handkerchief and reaching down for her gun.

The driver, Charlie Francis, called to the team, easing them down.

"I thought they caught the stage robbers." The passenger across from her sat up and stuck his head out the window. "There's three men on horses in the road."

"What is this, boys? A holdup?" Charlie shouted from the driver's box. "I ain't got nothing but passengers this trip, and that's the honest truth."

"You got something I want." The voice from the front pierced Maggie's heart. It sounded just like Cal's.

"What could I possibly have that you want, Cal McConnell?"

Charlie's voice was tinged with laughter. "Unless it's that little gal who's been crying like a watering can since we left Money Creek. I wondered if you were touched in the head for letting her go."

"I don't aim to let her go, Charlie."

"I'd be obliged if you'd take her off my hands so my passengers can travel in peace."

Maggie closed her hanging jaw and tried to swallow.

Cal appeared outside her window. Dust streaked his handsome face, and lather decorated his horse's neck and flanks. "Margaret Davis, you and I need to have a talk."

She couldn't move.

"What's the idea of leaving town without telling me?" The sun glinted off his blue eyes, and his dimple flashed, making her heart trip.

Her breath crowded into the tops of her lungs.

He vaulted out of the saddle and wrenched the door open. "Excuse me, gentlemen. We'll have you back on the road in a minute."

"See here, what if the young lady doesn't wish to go with you? This is most irregular." A beanpole of an elderly gentleman, owner of the third handkerchief, put his hand on Maggie's arm.

"Maggie, I don't mean to let you get away. I love you, and I mean to marry you."

Her words stuck in her throat, and she had to try twice to get started. "You—you can't. I lied to you. You don't even know me, not the real me." She gripped her hands together until they shook, afraid this wasn't real, afraid he hadn't really ridden after her.

"You want me to tell you what I know?" He shoved his hat back on his head and lifted his boot to the metal step below the door. "I know you're smarter than anyone gives you credit for and very good at your job. I know your laugh sounds like music and that sometimes you get lonely. I know you like blueberry pie better than any other, and that whenever you're missing your father, you touch your necklace. I know you fight everyone else's battles and think you're no match for your own. I know you love me and that you'll never be happy without me in your life."

Every word he said was true, and with every word, he restored a piece of her heart. His eyes glowed warm. "Do you want me to go on, because I have about a thousand or so other things I could tell you about yourself."

"Why don't you stop jawing and just kiss her?" Alec rode close. "It's hot enough to melt rocks out here."

Cal shot his brother a disgusted glare. "Nobody invited you on this trip. I'm doing this the best that I can."

"Your best is taking forever."

As if he agreed with his brother, Cal reached into the coach and spanned Maggie's waist with his hands. He drew her out the door and into his arms. "Maggie, say you forgive me and that you'll come back and marry me."

"Forgive you?" She could barely get the words out for his embrace. "I'm the one who needs your forgiveness. I never should've doubted you."

His grin widened. "Maggie, love, let's just forgive each other and be done with it all. Our new life starts here, right now." He lowered his head and captured her lips.

Maggie responded, pouring all her love and forgiveness into that kiss.

A thump on the ground beside them startled her. Charlie had thrown her bag off the stage. "You're putting me behind schedule. If you're done robbing this stage, I'd like to get back on the road."

When the coach had pulled away and Cal had taken Maggie up before him in the saddle, she leaned back and brushed a kiss across his cheek. "I knew it from the moment

I saw you. You *are* a stage robber."

Cal laughed and squeezed her tight. "I love you, Maggie girl."

He turned his mount north. Toward Money Creek. Toward home.

A Letter To Our Readers

Dear Reader:
In order that we might better contribute to your reading enjoyment, we would appreciate your taking a few minutes to respond to the following questions. We welcome your comments and read each form and letter we receive. When completed, please return to the following:

Fiction Editor
Heartsong Presents
PO Box 719
Uhrichsville, Ohio 44683

1. Did you enjoy reading *Maggie and the Maverick* by Erica Vetsch?
   ❏ Very much! I would like to see more books by this author!
   ❏ Moderately. I would have enjoyed it more if

   _____

   _____

   _____

2. Are you a member of **Heartsong Presents**? ❏ Yes ❏ No
   If no, where did you purchase this book? _____

   _____

3. How would you rate, on a scale from 1 (poor) to 5 (superior), the cover design? _____

4. On a scale from 1 (poor) to 10 (superior), please rate the following elements.

   ____ Heroine   ____ Plot
   ____ Hero   ____ Inspirational theme
   ____ Setting   ____ Secondary characters

5. These characters were special because? _____

_____

_____

6. How has this book inspired your life? _____

_____

_____

7. What settings would you like to see covered in future
   Heartsong Presents books? _____

_____

_____

8. What are some inspirational themes you would like to see
   treated in future books? _____

_____

_____

9. Would you be interested in reading other **Heartsong
   Presents** titles? ❏ Yes   ❏ No

10. Please check your age range:
    ❏ Under 18   ❏ 18-24
    ❏ 25-34   ❏ 35-45
    ❏ 46-55   ❏ Over 55

Name_____

Occupation _____

Address _____

City, State, Zip_____

E-mail _____

THE BLACKSMITH'S BRAVERY

A reformed saloon girl and decent markswoman, Vashi Edwards earns the opportunity to drive stagecoach, but blacksmith Griffin Bane fears for her safety—and his growing attraction—as the line becomes repeatedly targeted by robbers. Can The Ladies' Shooting Club catch the bandits and bring the stubborn couple together?

Historical, paperback, 352 pages, 5⅜" x 8"

Please send me ____ copies of *The Blacksmith's Bravery*.
I am enclosing $12.99 for each.
(Please add $4.00 to cover postage and handling per order. OH add 7% tax.
If outside the U.S. please call 740-922-7280 for shipping charges.)

Name _____

Address _____

City, State, Zip_____

To place a credit card order, call 1-740-922-7280.
Send to: Heartsong Presents Readers' Service, PO Box 721, Uhrichsville, OH 44683

Presents

Great Inspirational Romance at a Great Price!

Heartsong Presents books are inspirational romances in contemporary and historical settings, designed to give you an enjoyable, spirit-lifting reading experience. You can choose wonderfully written titles from some of today's best authors like Wanda E. Brunstetter, Mary Connealy, Susan Page Davis, Cathy Marie Hake, Joyce Livingston, and many others.

When ordering quantities less than six, above titles are $3.99 each.
Not all titles may be available at time of order.

HEARTSONG
PRESENTS

If you love Christian romance...

$12.⁹⁹

You'll love Heartsong Presents' inspiring and faith-filled romances by today's very best Christian authors...Wanda E. Brunstetter, Mary Connealy, Susan Page Davis, Cathy Marie Hake, and Joyce Livingston, to mention a few!

When you join Heartsong Presents, you'll enjoy four brand-new, mass-market, 176-page books—two contemporary and two historical—that will build you up in your faith when you discover God's role in every relationship you read about!

Imagine...four new romances every four weeks—with men and women like you who long to meet the one God has chosen as the love of their lives...all for the low price of $12.99 postpaid.

Mass Market 176 Pages

To join, simply visit www.heartsong presents.com or complete the coupon below and mail it to the address provided.